THE MIDNIGHT MURDER

Inspector Allan Germain thought he detected a Mafia-killing in the pointless assassination of a demented man who tried to blow up an airliner with a home-made bomb. His bureau chief was sceptical, so Inspector Germain took his holiday, beginning the very next day, and got on the trail of Joe Buono, a professional Cosa Nostra killer. He discovered that Buono was in Northern California to assassinate the City Attorney of San Francisco. But could Germain convince the Police Department?

Books by John Morgan
in the Linford Mystery Library:

MURDERERS DON'T SMILE

JOHN MORGAN

◆

THE
MIDNIGHT
MURDER

Complete and Unabridged

LINFORD
Leicester

First published in Great Britain in 1971 by
Robert Hale Limited
London

First Linford Edition
published 2000
by arrangement with
Robert Hale Limited
London

British Library CIP Data

Morgan, John, *1916 –*
   The midnight murder.—Large print ed.—
Linford mystery library
   1. Detective and myst
   2. Large type books
   I. Title
823.9'14 [F]

ISBN 0–7089–5680–7

Published by
F. A. Thorpe (Publishing) Ltd.
Anstey, Leicestershire

Set by Words & Graphics Ltd.
Anstey, Leicestershire
Printed and bound in Great Britain by
T. J. International Ltd., Padstow, Cornwall

This book is printed on acid-free paper

1

An Athletic Man

The flight that left Boston International Airport touched down in Chicago before the passengers could finish their breakfasts, but there was ample time if anyone were still hungry to have a bite at the lounge-restaurant at Chicago airport, providing they were booked on the Denver flight, because that flight was being delayed pending a minute search of the aircraft resulting from a telephoned bomb-threat.

There was no bomb aboard; there usually was no bomb on board, but for every four hundred crank-calls, there was one genuine threat, but it was rarely this one genuine telephone call that worried both the carrier and his insurance firm. What worried them to the point of an obsession was the bomb planted aboard an aeroplane that *no*

1

one telephoned in about.

It was this very real peril that had raised operating-costs for all the airlines; they had had to recruit and train squads of technicians to go aboard immediately after passengers disembarked, on the off-chance that one of the departed passengers had been a bomber.

None of this, as a rule, ever got much publicity. Even when the technicians went aboard they were dressed as ordinary maintenance crewmen. Also, enough time was allowed between touch-down and take-off so that this search could be accomplished without arousing either alarm or curiosity.

When a double-check was made, as with the Denver flight, causing a delay that was sure to arouse the interest, or the resentment, of the waiting passengers, it was commonly explained as a scheduling-error or something equally minor, the theory being that, psychologically, it was better to have passengers annoyed by what they usually denounced as the damned inefficiency of the airline, than to have them know the truth and desert *en masse*.

One of the passengers on the Boston flight who hadn't finished his breakfast aloft before touchdown in Chicago, was an athletic man, perhaps thirty-five years old, wearing dark-rimmed glasses, who had crisp, curly dark hair, a pleasant smile, and who dressed very well, although quite conscrvatively.

He finished his personal refuelling at the lounge-restaurant then strolled to one of the huge windows of the first-class waiting area and lit a cigarette while idly watching the bustle and orderly confusion out on the huge flight-line.

It was said that an aeroplane landed at Chicago every six minutes, and one lifted off every two minutes, although to a watcher it seemed those statistics should have been in seconds instead of minutes.

The athletic man put on tinted sunglasses, finished his cigarette and continued to stand at the window for a minute more, watching. One particular maintenance man held his attention. He was the last person to leave the Denver-bound Boeing, which was normal, but instead of heading in the direction of the airline company's compound, this man went in the direction of the passenger parking-lot, unbuttoning his company coveralls as he walked briskly along. Even that might not have held the athletic man's particular interest, except that the departing maintenance man walked faster the farther he got from the tarmac, and near a wire gate he looked back.

The athletic man turned from the window, located the stairway and went down towards the mezzanine-floor two steps at a time. From there signs pointed towards the parking area. He hastened out of the building into the acres of parked cars and went swiftly in the direction the maintenance man had taken. Except for one thing he might never have found the man; he had not got out of his airline company suit and was doing so when the athletic man saw him leaning against a car while kicking loose of the coverall. The athletic man strolled over, stopped as the maintenance man raised his eyes, unbuttoned his jacket, reached to adjust the dark glasses and said, 'Where did you put it?'

The maintenance man stood holding his coveralls. He was now attired in a rather flashy but expensive-looking set of threads. He was shorter than the athletic man, and older, perhaps as much as fifteen years older. 'Put what?' he asked.

The athletic man reached inside his jacket, brought his hand out gripping a revolver, reached into a jacket pocket with his free hand, brought forth a metal cylinder, and proceeded to screw the cylinder to the end of the revolver. 'The bomb,' he said, as the older man stared.

'You're no cop,' exclaimed the older man. 'What the hell is the gun for? Who are you, Mister?'

The athletic man ignored the questions to say, 'One more time, then you're dead: where did you put it?'

It took this long for the older man to realize his very genuine peril. He didn't even hesitate. 'In the airvent over Number Six seat in the First Class Compartment.'

An outdoor loudspeaker announced that passengers were boarding Flight 13 for Denver as the athletic man squeezed the trigger, then turned and made a smooth, broken-field run back through the hundreds of parked vehicles to the terminal building. There, hardly breathing as though he had exerted himself, he ducked into a pay-telephone booth, called the airline ticket office, told someone where the bomb was, rang off, adjusted his jacket as he left the booth and went confidently back to the lounge-restaurant.

An impersonal, tinned voice announced blandly that the boarding of Flight 13 Denver would be postponed for a few minutes, but that all passengers should remain in the upstairs lounge-area.

The athletic man had a cup of coffee and another cigarette while he waited. The lounge-restaurant was on the wrong side of the building; it was possible to see incoming aircraft, but not those lined up for departure. He could have sauntered back up to the big lounge window, but he was quite content where he was. Across from the landing area, but rather southward so as not to interfere with touchdown flight patterns, was the immense and orderly parking-lot. That, from time to time, held the athletic man's attention. But nothing unusual happened out there.

He hadn't expected anything unusual to happen out there.

Finally, Flight 13's boarding clearance was announced. The athletic man dropped a coin beside his coffee cup and went up to the lounge, down the enclosed ramp to the transport vehicle that took all passengers out to the waiting Boeing, and only when he, along with several dozen other passengers, mostly disgruntled, filed on through into the aeroplane, was there any interest shown in them at all. Two husky men in dark suits scanned each passenger who boarded. It was a routine scanning except that this time the two husky men were unsmilingly alert.

The athletic man had Seat Ten in the forward, or First Class, compartment. He polished his dark glasses, studied his fellow passengers dispassionately, picked out the one who did not look as though he could really afford to fly First Class, put his glasses back on, lit a cigarette and deliberately turned his seat so that he could see out of the porthole. He did not do what that watching man farther back was waiting for someone to do; show interest in the air vent over Seat Number Six.

Lift-off was usually exciting. This time was no exception. The aircraft's burners ran up to maximum lift-off power, the pilot released braking mechanisms and the aeroplane surged ahead for what seemed only a very short distance, then its nose rose and the vibrations ended as Flight 13, Denver, was airborne.

Once, it had been possible as one soared westerly from Chicago, to look down at neat fields of wheat and sorghums, dairy cattle and giant silos. In those days there had been a distinct feeling that all was well with the nation, plenty of food was being grown and harvested, thrift and good management lay on all sides, down there, and it took a long while just to fly out of Illinois.

The only thing visible from over thirty thousand feet in a pressurized cabin was a spindrift of filmy clouds, and where lay a rent, the faraway, patchy rural world that could have been the surface of the moon when viewed through the polluted atmosphere. It was no longer possible to feel kinship with those acres of golden grain, to feel pride in the glistening silos.

A stewardess came to ask if passengers cared for a cup of coffee. The passenger in Seat Ten, First Class, asked for a whisky sour. It was a bit early, still, the policy of the airline was to accommodate passengers, and also, even now, in the age when trouble aloft was negligible, there were still a great many people who lived in torment from liftoff to touchdown. Every airline had a liquor locker aboard its flights hotels and taverns might really envy.

There was very little movement among passengers aloft. It was not discouraged, but neither was it encouraged. In many cases, people got comfortable and slept.

Some smoked like furnaces, some had highballs, some smoked *and* had highballs. Others read or listened to the tinned music, and because the flight from Chicago to Denver was not long, there was no motion picture.

Turbulence, which had been objectionable in the old days over the Great Plains, was far below Flight 13. An apologetic little old lady in Economy Class got sick over the Great Plains, otherwise the crossing was uneventful.

A very attractive stewardess with auburn hair and green eyes hovered near Seat 10 in the First Class area, to point out the snow-tipped peaks of the Great Tetons to the athletic man. He was interested. She also addressed him as Mr Carlysle, a compliment he noticed at once. It may only have been company policy for stewardesses to read First Class passenger lists; if so there was certainly some good psychology behind it; everyone was flattered to be addressed individually and personally as though he were important to the airline.

But too, the attractive girl with green

eyes and auburn hair might have had a more private interest in Seat 10. He was a handsome man, obviously confident, capable, athletic, and he wore a solid gold wristwatch, along with his tailored suit, which would be excellent harbingers of affluence even if he hadn't been flying to Denver in the First Class section. Any woman would have thought him attractive, even if she'd been wearing a wedding-ring, which the green-eyed stewardess was not.

She also leaned down to direct his attention to the distant great sprawl of Denver when Flight 13 first began to throttle back in order to begin its miles-long approach to the landing field.

'The mile high city,' she told Seat 10, with a smile that would have melted stone. 'I live there. Well . . . another stewardess and I keep an apartment there, because we have to lie over usually a day or two before getting another flight out.'

Seat 10 was interested although he did not take down the address of the apartment, nor even the attractive stewardess's name. But he was interested because he had never before been in Denver. In fact, he had never before been in the State of Colorado. His interest lasted until the aeroplane landed and he went at once to ascertain that his one suitcase had been shunted to the southward flight to San Francisco, then he bought another First Class seat to this fresh destination, and sauntered off in search of a restaurant for the noonday meal. According to schedule he would be in San Francisco by mid-afternoon. From there the real adventure began. He had done a lot of flying but never before in a helicopter, and never before into the inaccessible Californian mountains. In fact, he'd had no idea California had inaccessible mountains. California had always seemed to him to be Los Angeles.

He booked himself on the San Francisco flight as Arthur Bennington.

2

Eagle's Eyrie

Any southward flight out of Denver over-rode mountains most of the way. They showed up better to viewers seated more than thirty thousand feet aloft, than did the plains and valleys. Also, it was possible to note the gradual difference in colour. Around Denver, in fact throughout the flight-pattern across southern Colorado, the mountains were heavily forested and dark green. Afterwards, they were not quite so green and the trees were fewer until, over the great, crumpled and barren slopes of Nevada, it was like viewing the desiccated, mummified carcass of a gigantic snake, instead of mountains. Everything was tawny-tan. Even the level land was parched and empty. It was a moonscape, but in brown instead of grey.

Across the Sierras though, into Northern California, the world greened up again. Arthur Bennington leaned to study the tiers of blue-hazed mountains north of San Francisco. He was seeing them for the first time, and he was also impressed that they were so vast and extensive. Well, people lived and they learned.

He settled back to buckle up when the little lighted sign gave its impersonal order, and paid no heed at all to the majesty of the sparkling bay far below, the sun-glittery city, or even the Pacific Ocean beyond, although most people who had made the crossing from Boston, on the Atlantic Ocean, would have felt *something* at this magic-carpet-crossing of a continent between breakfast and dinner.

It wasn't that much old-hat yet; two-thirds of all flight passengers were well able to recall how much longer such a flight had taken only a few years earlier. But Bennington was not a flight-buff.

When the aircraft came in over the steel-blue water as though it would land on waves instead of the runway, others held their breath or were thrilled. Bennington read a note from an inside coat pocket, memorizing its contents, and missed the greatest thrill of landing at San Francisco Airport altogether.

He could not have cared less.

The air terminal at San Francisco was a huge, rather unclean building of several levels not very different from London airport. It was noisy and crowded day or night. The city, at least suburbs of San Francisco such as Menlo Park and San Carlos which actually merged with Greater San Francisco, left one with an impression of being much closer to the civic centre than one actually was.

That didn't seem to concern Bennington either, as he retrieved his overnight bag and sauntered out of the huge building in search of an area reserved for private aircraft where a blue and white Alouette helicopter was to be waiting.

Finding the private-plane pad was harder than locating a blue and white helicopter. San Francisco Airport was built on a scale to accommodate future traffic it would not in all probability have to worry about for another ten years.

There were taxis, usually an eye-catching bright yellow in colour, hovering like motorized vultures, but Bennington did not succumb. He went instead to a high ramp that provided an excellent, and quite scenic, view of the surrounding area, located the area reserved for private aircraft and even picked out the blue and white helicopter. Afterwards, having esti-mated route and distance, he struck off through what would have been hot sunlight if the airport hadn't been located upon a spit of land that had saltwater off shore.

It was a long walk by almost any standards; more than a mile in fact, but Bennington never faltered. When he reached the helicopter a lounging man, tow-headed, red-faced and wearing dark green sunglasses, straightened up from a waiting slouch and smiled as he extended a hand for the overnight bag.

'Mr Harrison?'

Bennington nodded. 'Yeah. How late am I?'

'Not late at all,' said the tow-headed

man, turning to toss the suitcase into the rear seat of his Alouette. 'I was going to allow another ten minutes, then go hunting for you. It's a big airport. Well, if you'll climb in and lash up, we'll get airborne. It's still a long way and I'm supposed to set you down before dark.' The tow-headed man swung up smiling. 'No sweat though; in July the sun don't set up where we're going until pretty damned late. After nine o'clock, I think.'

Mr Harrison climbed in beside the pilot, buckled himself in, tested the plexiglass door to make sure it was latched, looked upwards and around through the helicopter's completely transparent bubble, without asking a single question or saying a single word. The pilot was an affable, loose-jointed, somewhat casually sloppy individual and probably would have talked if Mr Harrison had been the least bit loquacious, and if conversation aloft in a French helicopter had been practical, which it wasn't because of motor and rotor noise, so from lift-off until they were beating their way northwesterly away from Greater San Francisco, nothing was said.

For Mr Harrison, who had crossed the nation at great height, the rather lumbering, low-level helicopter flight offered a splendid opportunity to see Northern California's mountains. They looked like the Colorado Mountains, or, for the matter of that, just about any mountains he'd ever seen that had had trees growing all over them. A couple of times the tow-headed pilot pointed downward to name wide rivers, but when he was guiding his awkward craft above the permanent glacial ice of the Trinity Alps, he said nothing at all, as though Mr Harrison couldn't possibly be interested in anything that mundane.

Finally, heading in what could have been a more westerly direction although Mr Harrison had long ago lost all sense of direction, the pilot began losing a little altitude. He leaned without a word to point to a lake on the top of a spectacularly large cone-shaped mountain. Evidently this was their destination.

There was a large grassy meadow

completely encircling the lake. Behind it were giant trees; pines and firs, that went back up the higher slopes, topped out, and covered the far, downhill slopes of the extinct old volcano all the way down to where the forest seemed endless.

That mountaintop lake had what Mr Harrison thought had to be the bluest, blue water in the world. He had never seen such blue water before.

As the helicopter banked around the huge cone while the pilot studied the terrain below, Mr Harrison saw what looked like one of those parties he'd seen in Western movies winding its laborious way up the side of another mountain. It looked like perhaps six or eight riders, and a nearly equal number of mules with packs on their backs. He grinned to himself, gave his head a little shake, then, as the helicopter dropped lower and straightened for the descent, he made a final long study of the mountaintop with the blue lake in its centre. He'd never seen anything quite like it before.

His biggest surprise, though, came when the craft hovered no more than two feet above the meadow. The pilot shook his head as he reached for Mr Harrison's case. 'You've got to jump down. There's a federal law — no mechanised vehicles allowed in here. I can't touch down.' He leaned to fling open the plexiglass door and grin. Mr Harrison looked around, looked down into the grass, tossed out his case and jumped down. At once the prop-wash nearly swept him away as the tow-headed pilot began to lift clear.

Mr Harrison looked incongruous and felt it. He was dressed in very good taste for downtown Boston, or Chicago, or even for cosmopolitan San Francisco, but not at all for the top of an extinct volcano only God-knew-where in the mountains of Northern California.

He removed the dark glasses, polished them, then looked all around. A lumpy individual in a checked shirt and light coloured boots was strolling towards him from beyond the grassy meadow where forest-shade and fragrance looked particularly inviting. It was hot out there in the meadow, although at that altitude and with that exquisite lake, it shouldn't have been.

Mr Harrison replaced his glasses, waited for the lumpy man to reach him, then he said, 'Tell me something, Mario; what in gawd's name is he doing in a place like this?'

The lumpy man, grey and perhaps in his mid- or late-forties, grinned. 'How are you Joe-boy? You look fit, like always; still on that health-kick, eh? Well; each to his own, as *he* says, eh?'

Joe held out his arms. 'What is this, Mario; Shangri-La? A lake on a mountaintop. Why?'

Mario lit a cigarette and offered the pack. 'He likes it. He was always strong on this kind of stuff. Look at me; in a shirt I wouldn't be buried in. And these goddamned boots weigh a ton. Do you know something, Joe? This is on the level: There are *bears* up here. They raid the garbage pit every night or two.'

Joe dropped his arms, picked up the case and shook his head again, as he'd done in the helicopter. 'For Christ's sake,' he muttered in disgust. 'Okay, where is he?'

Mario led off back the way he'd come. He said nothing until they got into the shade of the forest, then he stopped and very carefully put out his cigarette. Joe watched, Mario acted apologetic, shrugged, and they started off again. 'No fires, Joe. He says no shooting, no fires, no drunks. It's good for the lungs and the digestion up here. It's communing with God, he says.' Mario jerked his head to indicate the blue-water lake. 'That's the bathtub. Joe; that goddamned water's so cold you're an hour just getting your breath back.'

'How long is he going to stay up here?'

'Who knows? He bought this place.'

Joe stopped dead. '*Bought* it? The top of a mountain in the middle of nowhere?'

Mario grumbled and walked on. 'He's waiting.'

A fair sized clearing had been made midway through the forest fringe. A chalet-type structure stood there; the kind called an A-frame, except that this one was taller at the peak and broader at the ground-level, with a lovely little shale-roofed porch running all along the front.

Joe admired it and Mario, who was a careful person, simply said, 'He had it built elsewhere and that guy with the blue-and-white chopper flew it in along with a couple of carpenters.' Mario shrugged, gazing forward. 'It's what's called a pre-fab A-frame.' Mario did not say he liked it, did not like it, thought the whole idea was preposterous, or that he admired the A-frame.

They crossed the last twenty yards and Mario stopped at the foot of some steps leading to the porch and pointed. 'Go on up.' He showed Joe a recessed button in a bit of A-frame siding. 'He knows it's you, but I push the button anyway. He'll meet you on the porch.'

Joe hesitated. 'Any idea what it is?'

Mario, the careful man, shook his head. 'You come one hell of a long way if he just wanted someone to play chess. Go on up . . . By the way, Ben and Rose are up here too.' Mario punched the button and Joe took the first step. Mario was below and behind him. Up above was Ben. If the purpose of getting him to this God-forsaken place had been liquidation it couldn't have been managed better.

The porch above didn't really offer any better view down through the trees towards the meadow and the yonder lake than looking back from the forest's edge offered, but there was some psychological reaction to admiring a view that heightened the sense of appreciation if a person were in the air.

Joe lit a cigarette and leaned on the railing. He'd left the case back near the stairway. Seeing that blue water like this, through trees and shadows, gave one the feeling of being hidden, or perhaps predatorily watching without being watched.

Otherwise, it was quite a setting; incongruous as all hell, but quite a setting. It somewhat resembled one of those calendar pictures some business establishments sent through the mail right after Christmas each year — the business establishments that didn't use naked girls on their calendars.

Joe stepped to the edge of the porch while he waited, and looked behind the house. Back there, the slope went up rather abruptly. More trees, some wild flowers and a lot of stone were visible all the way to the upper rim. Beyond that was just more blue sky.

Joe put out his cigarette in a hammered copper ashtray on the massive redwood table in the centre of the porch and arrived at the only conclusion he could have arrived at.

He remembered the sixty-five-foot yacht, and after that the damned island in the Caribbean — he got seasick every lousy trip down there he made. And now this. A man worth millions was entitled — fine — but for Joe Buono this place was for birds, or maybe monks who wanted to sit around all the time meditating. It wasn't even fit for lying low; a guy would end up talking to birds and *getting answers*. It was something like prison up here, the difference being that although a man could walk away, he'd never make it, not across all those lousy mountains and through all the trees.

It was an alien place, like an alien planet, and Joe Buono was a person who had to be entirely master of an environment, all its aspects, or he wouldn't stay in it. That was why he was such a success in his line of work in the world that lay hundreds of miles away from this damned quiet and spooky mountaintop.

3

The Man In Roman Sandals

The man who came through the immense, sliding glass door behind Joe Buono, had thick, protruding lips, very little greying hair, and a round body that went with his amiable, almost diffident light brown eyes. He looked like someone's delightful uncle, or maybe even a jovial young grandfather who could play the role of Santa Claus to perfection.

He was not an old man, perhaps fifty-five, but his soft body, thin hair, and general appearance made him seem older. He wore a beautiful blue diamond on his right hand, a platinum wristwatch on the opposite arm, and when he came forth smiling, hand extended, to greet Joe Buono, he was attired in a net, see-through shirt with short sleeves that exposed surprisingly hairy arms, and white cotton trousers above thick, Roman sandals.

Angelo Scarpino — it had originally been Scarpinato — was average height but that was not at once apparent because he was so round he seemed shorter. The pictures of him that had, from time to time, appeared in newspapers and magazines invariably showed him very properly, and conservatively, attired. Probably no more than a dozen people had ever seen him as he was now, when he motioned Joe Buono to be seated at the big redwood table. That had been one of Angelo Scarpino's fetishes — good clothing; nothing flashy at all. The kind of clothing bankers and brokers wore. Angelo Scarpino was also a professional man; that was the image he clung to, and it was also the image he dressed to emulate.

'How was the flight?' he asked Joe Buono, genuinely interested.

Joe said, 'Mind if I smoke, Mr Scarpino?'

The great hairy arms flew wide in a

gesture of generosity. 'Come on, Joe, you're like a son. Smoke if you like. It's bad for you, son, but smoke. I'll get matches. You got matches? Then light up, Joe.'

Buono did just exactly that, and on the exhale he said, 'It's quite a place, up here. Your own lake and forest — your own mountain.'

Angelo Scarpino beamed. He was, at times, an expansive person. 'Look at that sky, Joe; you ever see such a clear sky before? Taste that air, fresh like you never smelt before. Listen — so quiet here you can hear fish jumping in the lake. Joe, this is how men were supposed to live, eh?'

Joe inhaled, nodded and leaned upon the table. He was finally beginning to feel tired. It had been one hell of a long day.

Angelo Scarpino looked at him. 'Nothing happened on the trip?'

'A nut planted a bomb on my flight out of Chicago to Denver.'

Angelo Scarpino looked pained. 'There's getting to be so many of them in the world now, Joe. That's one of the reasons why I wanted to come up here where there is peace. Well, Rose is fixing up the guest-room for you and we'll eat together in a little while, Joe, then the helicopter will be here in the morning to take you back.'

Buono stubbed out his cigarette. He wouldn't be sorry to leave this place.

'Do you remember Carmine D'Angelo, Joe, the driver for old Sal Nitti back in Boston?'

Buono remembered. 'He was older than Mario and me; he used to pick up expense-money shooting pool.'

Scarpino smiled. 'That's him. Well, he did a foolish thing, Joe. He got hooked on heroin and when they arrested him down in San Francisco and put him in a cell, cold turkey, he spilled his guts in exchange for a dose.'

'I see,' said Joe Buono, who was a little puzzled. 'But Mario was already here, Mr Scarpino.'

The light brown eyes were warm and friendly. 'But it's not just Carmine, Joe. Mario will do that in time. It's bigger. Come on, Joe, give me credit for a little more brains than that; it costs money importing you. No, there is a City Attorney down in San Francisco who has been making a long, quiet investigation of the Cosa Nostra on the West Coast. That's who Carmine spilled his guts to. Now, Joe, I would guess that this City Attorney probably, by now, has quite a bit of background information. You see my point?'

'Yes, sir.'

Angelo Scarpino smiled. 'Take care of him for me, will you, son?' He put a thick envelope on the table between them. 'Expense money. Now let's go see how Rose is making out with the lasagna.' Scarpino arose from the table, leaned over the porch railing and called downward. 'Mario; come on, it's about dinner time. Mario? Find Benny and let him take over for a while, eh?' Scarpino turned back. The thick envelope had disappeared from the tabletop and Joe Buono was straightening his jacket. Nothing would ever again be said about that. Angelo Scarpino flapped his hands. 'You think it's unnecessary, keeping Mario and Benny here? You're probably right, Joe, but a few days back some people came up here on horses to fish in the lake. Harmless, but I feel better with Mario and Benny looking after things.'

They entered the house through the same large, sliding glass door. The fragrance of cooking spices filled the place. Joe's stomach rumbled. Angelo Scarpino waved at the elaborate furnishings as he padded along towards the kitchen. 'Had to bring it all in by air,' he announced. 'Nice, eh, Joe?'

It was, as a matter of fact, very nice. The inside of Angelo Scarpino's retreat had been given a rustic finish, but not too rustic. It was furnished in good taste too.

In the kitchen a sturdy woman in her late forties or early fifties with liquid large dark eyes, a great mass of grey-streaked black hair, and a tough-kindly expression, turned, flashed perfect white teeth and went over to Joe with both arms wide. Buono responded with his first genuine smile all day. He kissed her cheek, returned the hug, then fished in a jacket pocket for the tiny box he'd brought all the way from Boston, right after he'd been given his instructions where to go and who he was to see.

Rose Scarpino had been an exquisite girl, voluptuous and with the promise of very generous proportions later, and now was later, but she still had an exquisite smile. She opened the small box, lifted out the amethyst with the Holy Cross embedded in the back of the stone so that it was visible in front as though through a beautiful glow, and turned with her lovely eyes abrim. 'Joe, Joe, it's so beautiful.' She kissed him again. Mario clumping through from out front shattered the mood. Angelo made a small, hurrying gesture to his wife, then took Joe back to the sitting-room where Mario was lighting a cigarette and standing near a leather chair.

'Sit,' said Angelo, being a good host, which he usually was. 'Sit, and I'll get some wine. Mario, I explained things to Joe. Maybe there are details; I'll get the wine.'

After Angelo Scarpino left the room Joe arched his brows. 'What details?'

'Nothing,' said Mario, getting comfortable. 'Carmine just got stupid. If he'd come to Mr Scarpino, to me even, but he acted stupid, the cops picked him up and you know the rest of it.'

'Picked him up for what?'

'Addict. I don't know how they knew, but it wouldn't be hard to find out, would it?' Mario shrugged. 'Anyway, it's not Carmine, it's that Hale Buchanan.'

'The City Attorney?'

'Yes. Always it's somebody's going to boost himself into Congress or something by fighting the Mafia. You know, Joe . . . '

'Yeah, I know. Well, no sweat, is there?'

Mario didn't think so. 'Probably not. Take a few days though. You know San Francisco?'

Joe scowled slightly. 'Not very well.'

'Take a few days, get acquainted with it. Like any other town, Joe; look around, figure everything, make it good when you hit this guy, and make it good when you leave. Routine — if it's done right, eh?'

'Yeah.' Joe fished forth the envelope, slit one end and fingered through the money.

'Five thousand,' murmured Mario. 'It's

a bonus, but you were always Mr Scarpino's son he never had. Me, for Carmine, I get fifteen hundred.' Mario did not act envious; he wasn't. Mario was a careful man, and also a philosophical one. It was a good way to be, in life. 'Hey, what did Rose squeal about when I came inside a few minutes ago?'

'I brought her a cross of gold set in a stone. A necklace.' Joe smiled a little crookedly. 'You know how she is.'

Mario's dark eyes brightened. 'Yeah. She was depressed for a week when they said Saint Anthony was a myth. She has those little statues in all their cars, carries one in her handbag on aeroplanes. Speaking of aeroplanes, how was the trip?'

Joe put the envelope back and leaned in his chair. 'I could have picked up a hell of a good looking stewardess.' He acted pensive. 'Red hair and green eyes. She had a pad in Denver.'

Mario chuckled. 'Tough. Well, when you get back you can make up for it.'

Angelo Scarpino returned with glasses and a chilled bottle of wine. As he set them upon a low, carved coffee table he said, 'Joe, no electricity. We have our own generator up here. Cost six thousand, and then another thousand to get the exhaust rigged up so it wouldn't make any noise. Those workmen thought I was crazy.' Angelo handed round full glasses.

Joe was politely impressed but he had something on his mind. Mario sipped wine, watched the other two men, and kept silent. Angelo sank into a large chair and crossed pudgy legs, sandals flapping. He looked happy and content. He said dinner would be ready in a few minutes, then he loosened all over. 'Joe, that was a beautiful thing you did. You never forget Rose, do you?'

Joe was a little embarrassed. 'Nothing, really, Mr Scarpino. I just think she's wonderful that's all.'

Angelo nodded. 'Then what's on your mind, Joe?'

Buono put his half-empty glass on the coffee table. 'I was wondering about this City Attorney, Mr Scarpino.'

'I see.' Angelo studied the glass in his hand. 'Did anybody say anything to you in Boston when they sent you the orders to come to me?'

'No, sir. That's not what I meant. As far as I know no one back there is worried at all. But if they were, they wouldn't tell me, would they? I'm just a guy who travels a little now and then.'

That statement did not seem actually to relieve Angelo Scarpino, but he kept smiling. 'Okay, then what is it that worries you?'

'Well; just how much could this City Attorney know about the West Coast establishment? I mean, Mr Scarpino, will hitting him without getting his files be sufficient?'

Scarpino's light brown eyes ran to Mario then back to Joe Buono. 'That's not the point, Joe. Sure, he's probably got enough in his files to start a big stink — prosecute people, get a big newspaper spread as a crusader — but, Joe, the point is that we don't want to get all involved in trying to get whatever evidence the man has; it's too damned complicated, doing things like that. You get into trouble. You see, when this man is hit, it won't matter who takes his place or who sees what he's collected over the past few years. They'll understand. Anybody who tries it next gets the same thing. Like sending them all a polite warning. Those guys don't really want to make no trouble for the family; what they want is something that'll look good in the papers, something that'll make people want to vote for them. Well, Joe, no one wants to die, do they?'

Buono smiled and retrieved his glass of wine. 'No sir.'

Angelo Scarpino beamed. His wife had just appeared in the doorway. He rose and led the way. The diningroom was small, just large enough for the table, chairs, and a set of built-in mahogany shelves that held some of Rose Scarpino's lovely crystal. Joe Buono recognized the glassware from the yacht and from the lousy Caribbean island. It looked beautiful the way it caught and reflected yellowish light from the brass chandelier. It was a wonder Rose's crystal hadn't got broken, being taken from place to place. Maybe it had; maybe Mr Scarpino had replaced all that stuff a couple of times.

Joe held the chair for Rose and Mario waited patiently until all the others were seated, then he sat. Rose Scarpino made a lasagna that was out of this world. In fact, Rose Scarpino was the kind of cook people talked of and never really knew. She also happened to love cooking; even at the estate in Florida with two servants, Rose did most of the cooking. And she cooked as though she were preparing a feast for the family Rose and Angelo Scarpino had never had. It was as though Rose used cooking to compensate for something.

She was wearing Joe Buono's necklace with the crucifix embedded in the stone. It looked very nice, and so did Rose, in that yellowish soft light. She urged Mario and Joe Buono to eat, eat up, put some flesh on their bones, relax and bring pleasure to her by eating all the food she had prepared.

Joe and Mario couldn't, but Angelo

plunged in as though he could do it. He had been playing this game with his Rose for years; she'd cook enormous amounts of food, and Angelo would do his best to eat them.

4

'You Are Crazy!'

At issue, said Detective Inspector Allan
Germain, was not the corpse with the
hair-lined bullet through its heart. At
issue was who had done that, because the
corpse had been parolled from the Adult
Remedial Authority's sanatorium five
days before, and as well as Inspector
Germain could make it out, that dead
man, Foster Hellner, had no close
relatives anywhere near Chicago, and no
friends or enemies who had any idea he'd
been released. At issue, then, claimed
Inspector Germain, was who had discovered that Foster Hellner had planted his
bomb, and who had wrung its location
out of him, had killed him with a
silencered-revolver, .38 calibre, and who
had then telephoned to the Reservation
Desk of the airline.

To make his point Inspector Germain

held up a passenger-list for Flight 13, Chicago to Denver. 'Salesmen, people returning west who had been on holiday around Washington, a honeymooning couple, a pair of Englishmen sight-seeing.' Germain lowered the list to his desk-top. 'And one passenger travelling west under the name of Arthur Carlysle, who transferred off an Eastern Seaboard Airlines jet earlier incoming from Boston, who was listed on Flight 13 to Denver as Arthur Bennington. From Denver to San Francisco he was Mr Harrison. There is no trace of him by any of those names in San Francisco.'

The grey and mildly bored older man across the desk from Inspector Germain, nodded very stolidly. 'Okay, who was he?'

'Joseph Buono, a Cosa Nostra soldier — assassin.' Germain pocketed his copy of the Flight 13 passengerlist and rose behind the desk, he was a large-boned, lean man, mild in the face, blue-eyed and with light brown hair. 'My point, Captain, is that Foster Hellner can go to hell for all we care, as you pointed out this morning;

one less irrational and incurable murderous psychopath, and the world is that
much better off. But Joseph Buono is one
of the best assassins they have on the east
coast. That he somehow found out
Hellner tried to blow up his flight, is
interesting. It's also interesting that he
was incensed enough to kill Hellner. But
what I'd like your permission to do, since
I'm not presently assigned, is run this
thing down. Captain, a man like Buono
doesn't just casually cross the country.
He's on an assignment as sure as I'm a
foot high.'

'In Denver? That's one hell of a long
way out of our precinct, Allan.'

'Somewhere around San Francisco,'
corrected Germain, 'which is even farther
from our bailiwick.'

The captain looked pained. 'Allan,
what the hell are you talking about; you
couldn't possibly do a thing like this.
You're making no sense at all.' The
captain rose to his full thick and burly
height.

Allan Germain waited until his superior
was nearing the office door. 'Captain, I've

got twenty-one days of annual leave coming. I'd like to start taking it tomorrow. All I want you to do is to contact the San Francisco Police Department and get me cleared for their area. You've done it a hundred times before.'

The older man stood gazing back. 'You are crazy,' he growled. 'You want to spend your holiday trying to run down some punk; what kind of a vacation is that? Take my advice, Allan . . . You've worked pretty hard this past year . . . Take my advice and go up to the Maine Woods for some good trout fishing.'

Germain was calmly, quietly, adamant. 'Will you get me cleared for San Francisco?'

The captain's throat swelled and colour pumped into his face. 'Listen; what the hell, if one lousy Mafia assassin went through, and did us a favour with Hellner on the delay between flights; what are you trying to make it add up to? Okay, so he's on his way to the West Coast to ice some recalcitrant punk in the Cosa Nostra — let him.'

'And suppose he's on his way out there

to ice someone else — maybe the Commissioner of Police, or the Mayor of San Francisco, or the Governor of California?'

The captain stood gazing, then he said, 'Christ! All right. But I'll tell you something, Allan, when you come off annual leave I'm going to suggest that you have a complete physical — head to tail but mostly head. Whoever heard of a real professional acting like some zealous rookie? Go to San Francisco!' The captain slammed the door after himself.

Germain lifted the telephone, made arrangements to fly out of O'Hare Airport for San Francisco at midnight, then cleared his desk, called the 'morgue' for whatever else they might have found out about Foster Hellner, the psychopath who did completely irrational, disconnected and irresponsible things, and was told only a little more than the initial autopsy had revealed.

'Epileptic, among other things, Inspector, and if he hadn't stopped one today, he'd probably have stepped in front of a car next month or next year. Liquor undid about all the small good medical treatment had done him. We sent the slug along to your ballistics.'

'I know,' replied Germain. 'I've already got the report on that.'

'Well, we'll have the full analysis completed by tomorrow and sent over to you.'

Germain said, 'Thanks,' rang off, waited briefly, then dialled the Records Bureau. There was one thing he needed to bolster his conviction that the madman who had made and hidden the bomb on Flight 13, had done so upon his own initiative.

He did not get it from the Records Bureau. All they could tell him was roughly what he'd already dug up on Foster Hellner. But the clerk down there had a brilliant suggestion.

'Call the Adult Authority. Hellner's number was 609,006.'

Germain took that advice, and finally, close to quitting time, got a crisp medic who dug out 609,006's file and cleared his throat at city expense while he browsed through. Finally he said, 'Okay,

Inspector, here it is. Eliminating the technical terminology this man was first treated at city expense back in 1960. Inhibited to the point of withdrawal. Certified and released in 1962. Back with the Authority in late 1962, around Christmas time — same thing again, complicated with alcoholism.' The medic sighed. 'It's almost five o'clock, Inspector; all right if I sum up quickly?'

'Fine,' agreed Germain.

'This 609,006 was incurable. He kept coming back, but there really is no cure for his kind. They just simply can't cope.'

'Suppose someone tried to hire him to plant a bomb in a aeroplane?'

The medic cleared his throat again. 'I would say that unless he could be convinced the idea was his and not another person's idea, he wouldn't do it. But the hell of it is, Inspector, no one can accurately predict what one of these nuts will do. I see in his file where he was at one time a demolition expert in the army. Were you aware of that?'

Germain was very aware of it. 'It's in his police record, Doctor. Tell me, is there anything in his Adult Authority record that would indicate he had a grudge against aeroplanes? I'm trying to piece together his motivation as well as his movements, prior to having tried to blow up an airliner.'

'Well,' said the medic, sounding very pragmatic, 'I see nothing here that would indicate some particular animus, some polarization of his hatred towards anything in particular, aeroplane or anything else, but as I said earlier, Inspector, all the best of us can do is study them, try to catalogue them, and if we value our professional reputations, never make our predictions rigid at all. With this one, I would think he just had a hot-flash, as it were, perhaps from seeing an airliner on television, or perhaps when he saw one in a magazine. He was trained in demolitions. Maybe he didn't see a picture at all, perhaps he read of someone planting an explosive device on an airliner . . . We'll never know will we? He *is* dead, isn't he, Inspector?'

'Very dead, Doctor, and thank you very much.' Germain put the telephone down, glanced at his watch, shot to his feet and headed for the door.

It was neither a long nor a particularly hazardous drive to his apartment building where he showered, changed, and went out to his favourite restaurant, celebrating the first holiday meal by treating himself to a sirloin steak, a tossed green salad with genuine olive oil, not one of those blandly tasteless, thoroughly horrible safflower oils, and topped it off with a cup of very good coffee.

He still had six hours to kill.

There was a secretary in a law office not far from headquarters, Elke Jorgenson, who also had a flat in his apartment building. He decided against anything that complicated and strenuous, even though he had six hours to kill. Finally, he went back to his flat, packed, took his luggage down to the car and made a leisurely, time-consuming drive to the airport. There, he handed in the luggage, got his ticket, then went up to the observation deck, found an unoccupied chair, in fact a great many unoccupied chairs, got comfortable and fired up his pipe.

The captain was correct of course. It didn't make a lot of sense, a professional peace officer spending his own holiday, and his own money as well, sleuthing, particularly when he would be doing it in an area, in fact in a state, where he had absolutely no authority at all.

He'd had no such intention when he'd first read the reports about the corpse in the airport parking-lot. What had first piqued his interest had been the matter of someone, obviously not the bomber who was dead in the parking-lot, tipping off the airline about the bomb — exactly where it was cached.

The second thing that had intrigued him had been what the routine run-down on the passenger-list had turned up; Carlysle, Bennington, Harrison, Cosa Nostra assassin Joseph Buono, travelling through from Boston to the West Coast.

It had initially looked as though Foster Hellner might have planted his bomb to kill Buono — and of course a covey of innocent people as well — and that had been even more interesting, because if there was a schism in the Mafia family a lot of law-enforcement officers would dearly like to know about it.

But what it looked like now, to Germain, was that Buono had somehow-yet-to-be-revealed stumbled onto Hellner and his bomb, had taken Hellner out with a .38 bullet, and had then soared away on Flight 13 leaving a dead man in the parking-lot for no more reason than because he had been antagonized over Hellner choosing his particular flight to plant his bomb on.

To Joseph Buono the professional, killing someone like insane Foster Hellner meant nothing at all; no murder meant anything to professional assassins; not the act, not the corpse afterwards. The only thing they really considered, involved consequences. They would not kill unless they were absolutely satisfied they could do it clean. They also knew something that otherwise, only policemen knew; that when a total stranger walked up and shot someone to death, since there was absolutely no tie-in between victim and killer — one was dead, the other one would not talk at all, to anyone — the most stringent laws under the sun could not insure a conviction. Criminal lawyers tore witnesses to pieces every day by demanding to be shown that their client, the murderer, had ever seen, spoken to, known, or had any dealings whatever, business or social, with the dead person.

Murder consisted of two parts and both had to be present under the law to insure a conviction. The intent and the commission. When a man such as Joe Buono put someone on ice, they committed the act of murder. If they were apprehended, the prosecution had to prove beyond a reasonable doubt that they had intended to commit murder.

Very, very few professionals were apprehended in the act, but those that were, hardly knew their victim's name; proving any kind of association was impossible because none actually existed. There was obviously no intention.

Allan Germain knocked out his pipe, yawned, got to his feet and stood a while sniffing the polluted night air of Chicago, and took comfort that New York's night air smelled worse.

It was ten o'clock, he was drowsy, somewhere overhead airliners swooped in, lights flashing, and other airliners literally sprang upwards from earth boring holes in the moonless firmament, going aloft.

Germain went downstairs for coffee and a roll. He wasn't hungry but eating might help him stay alert. He hoped to sleep all the way across country to the West Coast.

Somewhere, far off, a siren wailed. Germain listened, then stood one last moment gazing up at the soiled sky wondering if, somewhere, there wasn't a place where people not only had no sirens, but better still, had no need for sirens.

He trooped down the stairs. There was no such place. There never had been and there never would be, as long as fifty or a hundred, or a hundred thousand or a million people ganged all together to make a city.

5

By Process Of Elimination

San Francisco at dawn, especially from the air, looked large, grey, impersonal and hostile. Most cities looked that way to people winging towards them before sunrise, more so if the viewer was a stranger. Inspector Germain had been to the West Coast before several times, but only once to San Francisco, and that had been to escort an extradited embezzler back to Chicago; an overnight stay.

What he needed first was a shower and a shave, then a change of clothing. Fortunately, San Francisco was a veritable honeycomb of hotels, motels, apartment buildings and rooming houses. Germain went to a hotel that was conveniently close to the huge headquarters building of the San Francisco Police Department, spruced up, then went in search of a decent restaurant. San

Francisco was just as noted for its restaurants as for its hotels. By the time Inspector Germain checked in with the San Francisco Detective Bureau, and had accepted the invitation of a Sergeant Moore to have coffee with him, Germain had efficiently established himself. He had a place to sleep, a place to eat, and now he worked at establishing a rapport with a San Francisco homicide cop in order to have a contact.

Reginald Moore was a large, powerful man with baby-blue eyes, who had to be at least forty, to have achieved his rank and standing with the San Francisco Police Department, but he did not look it. He was a very good detective, too, although Inspector Germain could only guess about that as he sat in Moore's office explaining what had brought him to the West Coast. Sergeant Moore listened, sipped coffee, and when Germain was finished explaining, Sergeant Moore's eyes twinkled.

'I'd say your captain was probably right. Not about the jurisdiction, that'll be no problem, but about a cop spending his vacation — and cash — trying to track down a criminal. You didn't know Foster Hellner by any chance, or this Joe Buono?'

Germain hadn't. 'It's nothing personal, Sergeant. It's a strong hunch. Buono didn't have to kill Hellner. He didn't even have to continue to Denver on Flight 13. A later flight would have got him out there the same day. But in back-tracking Buono, it came out that he probably had worked out his schedule so there would be no delay anywhere along the line. What does that suggest to you?'

'What you said; it was a schedule.'

'And he was to meet someone here in San Francisco, Sergeant, to complete the schedule.'

Moore thought a moment. 'Boston to Chicago to Denver to San Francisco; Inspector, suppose this Joe Buono wasn't stopping in San Francisco; suppose this was another touchdown before he took off for some other place?'

Inspector Germain beamed. 'That's what we have to know, isn't it, Sergeant?'

Moore studied the other man a

56

moment, then smiled and reached for a telephone. 'Okay, Inspector,' He contacted someone named Arch and gave specific orders for Arch to check out the airport for the date Germain supplied. 'See if you can get a wire-telephoto of Joseph Buono who is a Cosa Nostra assassin . . . Yeah, Buono is our target. Get back to me as soon as you can, Arch.' As Sergeant Moore put aside the telephone Allan Germain lit a cigarette, then got to his feet.

'You'll have your own work to do, Sergeant,' he said. 'I'll explore the city for a few hours then check back.'

Moore was agreeable, and saw his Chicago visitor out. He suggested places of interest in San Francisco such as the Top of the Mark and of course Fisherman's Wharf, for Germain to see, but the first place Germain went was by taxi out to the airport. He had a photograph of Joe Buono too; he had no authority to press a private investigation and his impression of Sergeant Moore was that he would not appreciate it if an out-of-state officer did that.

Germain's second view of the air terminal, long after sunup the second time, confirmed his earlier impression that it was a worn, heavily used place that probably no amount of maintenance could keep looking clean and inviting.

He did not have in mind trying to pick out the detective named Arch from the hundreds of wandering people. What he had in mind was to look the place over, get the feel of it, and perhaps try to imagine where Joe Buono had gone from here.

He could have gone anywhere under the sun. There was every imaginable airline represented at San Francisco Airport. There were also every imaginable variety of human being there.

Reservation and ticket counters were side by side in endless rows, while between them a huge cement rotunda, larger than most skating rinks, sent echoes upwards towards the needlessly high ceiling, from all those scurrying feet.

It would have taken several detectives to canvass the airline reservation counters, and it could scarcely be expected that a clerk would remember one particular man. The harassed clerks would not have looked kindly on being taken away from their busy counters to dig up an old passenger list either, but what was even worse from Germain's view, was that he had no first name for Mr Harrison, and after viewing the swarm of people who infested San Francisco Airport on just one mid-week morning, he knew that every passenger-list for the past year would have at least one Harrison on it.

He strolled out front to the elevated cement ramp where passenger-cars and taxis came and went endlessly, and considered the crispness of the air and the clearness of the atmosphere, two unusual natural attributes in most cities in summertime. Off to his right lay the lagoon, and farther away, a greater expanse of blue-grey water where jumbo-jets, trailing black streamers, were letting down for landing.

On his left, partially obscured by a jutting corner of the cement air terminal building, were the private aircraft, gaily coloured, tied in place because San Francisco was a windy city even in midsummer, and very numerous. It looked as though half the population of San Francisco belonged to the private-plane set. But in mid-week that area down there was an island of serenity compared to the frantic noise and haste inside the main air terminal building.

Germain strolled down off the high ramp to the open area below and with no real reason for doing so, went over where the private aircraft were parked. He was not an airplane enthusiast but there was such a variety in this area anyone would have been interested. There were even several amphibious aircraft, a number of antique warplanes, obviously the property of ardent hobbyists, one with a shark's teeth painted on its engine nacelle, and a line of small, frail-looking autogyros, oneman vehicles.

There were a few people about. Germain's impression was that although some were private owners, mostly they were charter-plane owners.

It was possible that Joe Buono had

taken a charter flight. Germain strolled among the rows of aircraft speculating about that. If he had, then his destination had been somewhere within the environs of San Francisco, perhaps, or maybe farther afield, to some nearby town or village, but in any case it hadn't been, as Sergeant Moore had implied, onward to some other distant place, perhaps the Orient or South America, and that would narrow things down for Germain.

He leaned upon a silvery steel post that held a high, arched, mercury lamp, and watched two men a dozen or so yards away in earnest conversation. One was husky, very casually, almost indifferently, attired, the other was in a dark suit and was also sturdily built.

If Sergeant Moore's man was inside checking things out then perhaps Germain could expedite circumstances by doing the same in the private aeroplane area. The only thing that prompted this thought was hope that Buono hadn't gone on, perhaps overseas.

But he did not do any canvassing. Another thought came, and he liked it better, so he re-traced his steps back to the main building, found a switchboard and put in a collect-call to his captain back in Chicago. As soon as the contact had been made and Germain had identified himself, the captain said, 'Why should the City of Chicago have to pay for this call. You're on holiday, Allan?'

Germain's answer was basic. 'Because I'm doing the City of Chicago a favour, trying to find the man who killed a sterling citizen.'

'Hell,' grumped the captain. 'All right; what do you want?'

'The name of any Cosa Nostra people out here in the San Francisco area who are in trouble.'

'They're *all* in trouble,' exclaimed the captain. 'That's their line of work. But okay; where do I get back to you?'

Germain gave Sergeant Moore's name and department and rang off. It was a hunch and a thin one, but he thought it had a better chance of being worthwhile than spending the balance of the day talking to flight-buffs.

He took a taxi back into the central

part of town in search of a decent restaurant, found one, was outrageously flirted with by the readheaded cashier, but otherwise enjoyed his meal, and the frail hope he was beginning to entertain that Joe Buono might not have gone much farther than San Francisco.

By two o'clock in the afternoon he was back in Sergeant Moore's office where he received a careful appraisal and a verbal summary of what Moore's man had turned up at the airport. Sergeant Moore, who had been friendly and a little patronizing in the morning, was discernibly different in the afternoon. His reason for this subtle change did not become apparent right away.

'Your man Harrison-Buono may have flown out,' stated Moore, 'but it'll take more time and effort than we put into it this morning to confirm that. My man turned up sixteen Mr Harrisons, all on the same day. By process of elimination we can eventually trace them all down. But the question is: How much time do we have?'

Germain had no idea. 'Maybe none at all, Sergeant. I'm guessing that when someone sends for an assassin they do it because they want someone's mouth closed, or to punish someone. In either case I think they'll want things done without a lot of delay. On the other hand, this is all pure guesswork.'

Moore picked up a legal-sized piece of yellow paper and handed it over. 'From your boss in Chicago,' he said. 'It's a list of our Cosa Nostra *capos* out here. As you'll see, he gives an F.B.I. summary of who might need an outside killer. Of the four names, only one fits. While I've been waiting for you to come back, I had some spade-work done on that one individual. Incidentally, I've racked him a couple of times myself, so I have personal reasons for believing that what my enquiries turned up is probably true. He is in trouble with the Internal Revenue Bureau. The F.B.I. may consider that serious, but then the F.B.I. considers any infraction of federal statutes serious, while down here on my lowly level, I don't think anyone, least of all a Cosa Nostra chieftain, would be foolish enough to think that knocking off an income-tax-fraud investigator would solve any difficulties. That kind of trouble, people take care of through lawyers.'

Germain listened and read at the same time. When he had finished with the written report he pocketed it and got comfortable in his chair. 'You're right,' he said to Moore. 'That's not the kind of trouble I had in mind.'

Moore's expression of respect lingered. He evidently felt that he did not have a travelling-salesman-type of big city detective on his hands, whatever he might have thought about Allan Germain earlier in the day. 'I've put a man to checking those other three *capos*. But I doubt that we'll turn up anything; out there, we have our own intelligence unit. If there was a rumble in the offing they'd know about it. I contacted them, and they had no information of big trouble. However, there was one item: A minor member of one of the local families named Carmine D'Angelo was picked up on a narcotics charge, and left a day and a night in the cells, cold turkey. He offered to give information in exchange for a jolt.'

Germain pondered, and came up with a logical conclusion. 'If he's on someone's list, they wouldn't bring in a specialist like Buono.'

Moore conceded that. 'Doesn't seem probable. From what I was told D'Angelo's small pumpkins. His kind is seldom missed; he could be iced by anyone hungry for a thousand dollars, or even less. But for the time being no one can reach him. The City Attorney's got him in the maximum security ward.'

'Wringing him out?'

Moore nodded. 'The City Attorney's a guy who's got a thing about the Mafia. He's got a full-time assistant who works on nothing else.' The sergeant looked sardonic. 'I'm a cynic, Inspector. Maybe it's all on the level, and maybe it's a springboard to the State Legislature, or something bigger.'

Germain wasn't listening. If the list from Chicago was useless, and if the local police intelligence unit knew of no trouble within the local Cosa Nostra, this junkie the City Attorney was keeping under wraps might be Germain's best bet. Anything was better than sitting around Reginald Moore's office speculating and drinking coffee.

He rose. 'Can you get me a clearance to see the City Attorney's information?'

Moore nodded without any hesitation. 'Sure. Tomorrow, maybe?'

Germain smiled. 'This afternoon, maybe?'

Sergeant Moore grunted and reached for the telephone.

6

A Warm Trail

The clearance presented no trouble, but when Inspector Germain reached the maximum security tank of City Jail a dapper young Jewish lawyer by the name of Cohn was waiting to act as escort. He couldn't have been there to act as bodyguard, he was too frail for that.

Cohn was one of the City Attorney's bright young men. He couldn't have been out of law school more than a year or two. Germain knew the type because Chicago also swarmed with them.

But Cohn proved affable and efficient. He had arranged all the clearances for Inspector Germain. The two of them went through the steel, white-enamelled door into the maximum security area with little more than a pleasant nod from the big, black, unarmed officer on duty. It was so easy Germain was impressed. Of course the reason gaining entrance had been so easy was that it had been arranged in advance, but there was another small item: Almost anyone could walk *into* a maximum security prison. They were photographed while entering and they were just as securely locked inside as any prisoner, once they passed the door. After that, between teletypes, computers, and telephones, while the visitor visited, he was checked out so thoroughly that before he was allowed out again, even the big black uniformed officer at the white door knew his marital status, armed service serial number, and police rating.

Carmine D'Angelo was brought to an interrogation room. Cohn and Germain were already seated, waiting. D'Angelo was a pale-skinned man with great dark eyes and thinning dark hair. He looked to be a nervous wreck. He also looked sullen, but Germain had dealt with every aspect of sullenness. He gave D'Angelo a smoke and lit it. He did the same. Only Lawyer Cohn declined. He did not smoke, he said, a bit loftily it seemed to

Germain, and D'Angelo glowered at him.

'What's worse, picking brains or smoking; being a lawyer-fink, or using tobacco?' D'Angelo dismissed Cohn with that one statement and that one withering black look. Then he turned to Germain. 'Who are you?'

'Inspector Allan Germain of Chicago.'

D'Angelo considered that. 'Chicago? What the hell's that got to do with me? I haven't been near Chicago in five years.'

Germain smiled. 'Nothing to sweat over. It's probably a good thing you haven't, too. By any chance have you ever heard of a man named Joseph Buono?'

D'Angelo's brilliant black eyes remained unblinkingly on Germain for as long as it took to inhale, then exhale. 'Yeah, I've heard of him. So what?'

'Someone out here sent for him. He left Boston the day before yesterday and arrived here by way of Chicago and Denver.'

'Okay,' said D'Angelo. 'So he arrived here.'

Germain continued to be amiable. 'I know him too. Now why would one of the best assassins in the business be summoned out here from Boston, D'Angelo?'

Again the black eyes in their pasty setting burned brilliantly against Allan Germain for as long as it took to inhale smoke and blow it out. 'Me?' he murmured. 'Is that what you're thinking? They sent for Joe Buono to ice me?'

Germain shrugged. 'Damned if I know, but I can tell you this much, if the rumour is true that you filled in the City Attorney in exchange for a fix, D'Angelo, you know what your chances are as well as I do. Better, even. Now listen a moment; I want Buono. If I can get him before they turn you out of here, you'll have a head-start. I'll buy you that running time. But I can't do it unless I know where to find Buono, can I?'

D'Angelo didn't use the metal ashtray which was bolted to the metal table. He deliberately flung his cigarette stub into a corner to lie and smoulder, and burn a stain. 'Joe Buono,' he mumbled, obviously thinking private thoughts. He suddenly brightened. 'If you got him you couldn't hold him. There's no law says a man can't fly from Boston to 'Frisco.'

'Sure isn't,' agreed a very amiable Inspector Germain. 'He killed a man named Hellner in Chicago on the way, though, and back there we have very strict laws about killing people. I can hold him, don't worry about that, D'Angelo, but first I've got to find him. Where is he?'

D'Angelo slumped and crossed his legs. 'I don't know. I used to know him, years ago back east. I was older than him and the other kids in the neighbourhood. They looked up to me. That was a hell of a long time ago.'

Germain got the conversation back where he wanted it with a question. 'He didn't come out here for his health. He was on a tight schedule. Listen, D'Angelo, maybe he isn't here to hit you at all, I'm only guessing about that, but — '

'Yeah, you're only guessing — in a pig's ear. Don't give me this I'm-just-a-dumb-cop-trying-to-do-my-duty-routine.'

Cohn, sitting perfectly still except for small, quick eyes, waited for Inspector

Germain's reaction to this. If he expected indignation he must have been disappointed because Germain yawned, then tossed the packet of cigarettes on the table nearer D'Angelo. Actually, Germain had never cared much for cigarettes. He was a pipe smoker.

D'Angelo winnowed out another cigarette, waited until Germain also tossed over the booklet of paper matches, then he inhaled again, tipped up his face and blew smoke at the pastel ceiling. 'Christ! I screwed up but good. Okay; do you know Angelo Scarpino?'

Germain nodded. 'From the newspapers only. He's head of a Florida family, isn't he?'

'That's right. But he's bought a place up in the mountains north of here a few hundred miles. Joe Buono is someone he recruited years ago, when Scarpino was connected with a family in Massachusetts.'

Germain gazed at the black-eyed, pasty-skinned man a moment while fitting this into what he already knew, and suspected. 'Where, exactly, is this place Scarpino bought in the mountains?'

D'Angelo said, 'I've never been there, but a guy I know, Mario Spina, who's been Scarpino's bodyguard for about six years, told me it was somewhere on top of a damned mountain. That sounds kind of crazy don't it?'

Germain didn't think it sounded especially crazy but he agreed. 'Yeah. Where can I find Mario?'

'Not unless you also find Angelo Scarpino,' exclaimed D'Angelo.

Germain slapped his legs and shot up out of the chair with a look towards the City Attorney's man. 'Let's go,' he said, and as Cohn rose, straightening his sharkskin coat, Germain said, 'D'Angelo; anything I can do for you on the outside?'

The prisoner studied Germain a moment, then made a downward-drooping smile. 'Yeah. Get him before they put me out of here. But then they'll use someone else. Okay, cop, good hunting. Cohn? Tell Mr Fixit I'm going to need help in a couple of hours. Okay?'

Cohn nodded, and as he followed

Germain out of the little room, past the stone-faced guard in the glistening corridor, he said, 'I can't understand how people who have seen what that stuff does to other people can turn right around and use it themselves.'

Germain didn't even look at his escort as he said, 'I'll bet you can't understand it, Mr Cohn. Look, I want to see your boss. Can it be arranged?'

'Sure. He'll be back the day after tomorrow. He's in Sacramento attending a conference of prosecuting attorneys.'

'What I need, Mr Cohn, I need today.' Germain halted near the desk of the amiable big black uniformed officer and waited until the white steel door was opened. 'I want to know within the next hour or two exactly where I can locate Angelo Scarpino.'

Cohn smiled. 'I can show you on a map within the next fifteen minutes. How's that?'

Germain smiled benignly at the shorter man. 'Perfect. Lead the way to a map.'

It was more difficult locating a map of the country north of San Francisco than it was for Cohn to finally pinpoint Angelo Scarpino's extinct volcano. The reason was simply that in metropolitan San Francisco not very many people were enthusiastic about mountain tops. They found the map at a sporting goods store, and true to the Californian ethos, it was not just a utilitarian, everyday map, it was a thing, actually rather clever, made in bas-relief so that all the north country mountains, valleys, river-canyons and glens, were extruded someway from beneath, with what Inspector Germain assumed was true fidelity. Cohn knew the mountaintop because the City Attorney had showed it to him on one of these bumpy maps. Allan Germain bought the map, thanked Mr Cohn for his valued assistance, and headed back for Sergeant Moore's office, where he got precisely the kind of reception he would have given Moore, back in Chicago, if their positions had been reversed.

Moore allowed the map to be laid out atop his desk. He looked from it to Germain, then followed the rigid finger over tiers of mountains to the particular one Germain said was where Angelo Scarpino had his new hideaway.

'Well,' conceded Sergeant Moore, 'if a man were seeking a hideaway, I don't see how he could do any better, do you?' But Moore did not want an answer to that question; he had another one. 'Why Angelo Scarpino?'

'Because Joe Buono, according to the City Attorney's man, D'Angelo, was close to Scarpino, and because if what I've read about Angelo Scarpino is only moderately accurate, he could very well be the man who would use Buono for an assassination.' Germain straightened up from long consideration of the map. 'And also for one other reason. What other Cosa Nostra people out here on the West Coast are involved in anything that might require the services of a professional like Buono?'

Moore shrugged. 'Okay, none of the local chieftains. But what makes you so sure Scarpino is involved in anything? After all, he's not even a local chieftain. For all you know he's on holiday and likes mountaintops.'

Germain smiled. 'Then why would he import Joe Buono? Possibly he got orders from the east to take out some local capo.'

Sergeant Moore threw up his hands. 'Okay. But there are an awful lot of suppositions in this, Inspector.' He gazed at the map. 'And up there you'll be in the territory of some cow-country sheriff. You may get cooperation, but I wouldn't want to bet on it. Those guys like all the glory. They're elective people, remember.' Moore stepped over and frowned at the map again.

'You see that dotted line? Well, beyond it for a good many miles you'll be operating within the territory of a real prima donna of a cow-country lawman. We've had an occasional brush with him. He's an egotist and he's overbearingly dictatorial. He is also jealous as hell of outside law officers.' Moore stepped away from the map and smiled. 'I don't mean to dampen your enthusiasm.'

Germain said, 'I'm sure you don't, Sergeant. I'm sure you don't.' He picked up the map and rolled it as best he could. 'Don't wait up for me tonight, I'm going back out to the airport and see about hiring an aeroplane to fly me over that country — maybe even Scarpino's mountaintop.'

Moore thought a moment. 'You might as well drop a copy of your police manual as you swing low over his tent, or whatever he has up there, Inspector. Men like Angelo Scarpino are damned good guessers. A reconnoitering aircraft will tip him off as surely as though you'd used a bull-horn to announce your arrival.'

Germain was not exactly a novice, even though he had never been involved in anything quite like this case before. But training and instinct never really let a man down, providing he kept his head and his nerve. Moreover, Germain had no intention of doing anything more alarming than studying the terrain, for some way to reach Scarpino's sanctuary by rented car.

He left Sergeant Moore's office with his map, heading for his hotel, an early dinner, and perhaps later, if it wasn't too late by the time he got round to it, another drive out to that private-plane area of San Francisco Airport to see about hiring one of those charter pilots for the following day.

7

Overflight

San Francisco Airport by night was just as busy as by day, but the lights made it seem more elegant. It would ordinarily have been hard for Inspector Germain to stand on the cement causeway where the taxi dropped him, looking out over the miles of macadamized runways with their red, green, white, and even dark purple, lights, and not feel a thrill.

Great airliners were lifting off without any more delay between departures than there had been during broad daylight. The place was truly an international airport.

Germain sauntered back down where the lighted field showed those colourful rows of private aircraft. A large blue-and-white helicopter was being secured in place by that tousle-headed, indifferently-attired man Germain had

81

noticed earlier in the day. He would have gone over to strike up a conversation but a handsome, younger man looking unusual in a crew-cut, military-type haircut, smiled as Germain walked past. The younger man was standing beside a glistening twin-engined Piper Apache aircraft. 'Looking for a nightflight?' he called.

Germain turned, considered the face, the aeroplane, and walked back. 'No, but I'm looking for a charterflight northward over the mountains tomorrow. Is that up your alley by any chance?'

The young man stuck out a powerful hand. 'Jack Skinner. It's right up my alley.' After they shook and Germain had said his name, the charter-pilot turned and laid an affectionate hand on the twin-engine aircraft. 'This is Dolly, Mr Germain. Between us, we can take you over any mountain up in the north country you want to look at.' Jack Skinner turned back, losing his smile. 'Do you have co-ordinates — anything in particular you want to see? That's a big country, and it's rugged.'

Germain looked for the blue-white mercury lamp, took his map over there and spread it upon the tarmac with Jack Skinner bending over. Germain did not pinpoint Scarpino's mountaintop, he included the entire area in the sweep of his hand as he told Skinner what he wanted. The younger man started bobbing his head before Germain had finished speaking.

'Duck soup,' he said. 'What time do you want to leave in the morning?'

Germain straightened up. 'How is eight o'clock?'

Skinner's grin returned. 'The best time to fly out of here.'

The tousle-headed man sauntered past. Nodded amiably to Germain, then grinned at Skinner. 'Got a live one, eh? Okay; the beer's on you tonight.' He walked on.

Skinner looked a little embarrassed but Germain wasn't offended even before Skinner said, 'It's just a sort of joke among the charter pilots, Mr Germain. When one of us gets a charter the others rag him a little.'

'And he has to stand the drinks,' said Germain, stooping to retrieve his map. 'You're welcome to keep this thing if you'll need it,' he said, and Skinner shook his head.

'Ours aren't as elaborate but I choose their accuracy in preference. Thanks all the same.'

'Would you like something binding in advance?' asked Germain, and the pilot shook his head.

'Afterwards will be just fine.'

Germain nodded, looped the rolled map under his arm and headed back towards the cement causeway up above, where there was a hack-stand. He turned after he got up there for another look around the night-lighted airport. His charter-pilot had been hurrying along, evidently on his way out of the airport area, and that tousle-headed man hailed him. As Germain watched, those two came together, then turned and walked along a short distance together. Then, suddenly, the tousle-headed man stopped short and turned. After this he and Germain's charter-pilot spoke a little more before walking onward again. Germain paid little attention. Probably, the tousle-headed man who had been over by the blue-and-white helicopter had been envious that Skinner had got a passenger who wanted to spend the entire morning in the air.

Germain went along to the taxi-stand, caught a cab and headed for the hotel. He wasn't tired, hc felt elated and pleased with himself.

Of course he was doing all this on nothing more, really, than a hunch. The connection between Scarpino and Joe Buono fitted perfectly, but all Germain really had, was confirmation that Buono had not used San Francisco as a stop-off, as he'd used Chicago and Denver.

Well, perhaps he had a little more, if Carmine D'Angelo's word was worth anything, which it probably wasn't under ordinary circumstances, but which Germain felt it was this time. But he was certain Scarpino, if he were indeed the capo to receive instructions from the Council back east to liquidate someone, would never have gone to all the expense of bringing in someone like Buono to hit a person of no more importance than D'Angelo. Big-time Mafia chieftains were just as cost-conscious as any other businessmen.

But — if it wasn't to be D'Angelo, who was Buono supposed to kill? That intrigued Allan Germain throughout his shower, and later, when he was smoking his pipe, feet cocked upon a windowsill, waiting for drowsiness to arrive.

It could be any of the local *capos* and that would make sense because the Mafia Council would never allow one local chieftain to take out another one. That was how vendettas were started and whatever else the Cosa Nostra was, it shunned anything like the old-time gang-war type shoot-outs of Prohibition days.

Who did that leave? Germain ran a number of suggestions through his head but none of them could stand the cold analysis of second-thought.

He went to bed, finally, just short of midnight, and slept like a child. Such a thing was always possible in San

Francisco where nights were cool no matter how hot the days were, thanks to all that wetness out there in the Bay.

In fact, he slept so well that he barely awakened in time to shower, shave, jump into his clothes and call down for a taxi to be waiting when he finished a fast breakfast of coffee and one sweet roll.

San Francisco on a summertime morning, early, was just beginning to rumble like a large city, but the roads were less congested than they would be an hour later, so the drive to the airport was made smoothly and in good time.

Jack Skinner was waiting, smoking a cigarette and sipping jet-black coffee from a paper cup. When he saw Germain walking forward, Skinner's face broke into the kind of smile that had to be mostly relief. He finished the coffee, chucked the paper cup into a green barrel nearby, then went to the off-side of his aeroplane and opened the door for Inspector Germain. Before he closed it he pointed to the lap-and shoulder-harness. Germain obediently buckled himself in. When Skinner climbed in on the opposite side and tossed a clipboard with a check-list on it into the rear compartment, he said, 'If there are any particular instructions, or anything like that you'd like to clear with me, now would be the time, Mr Germain, because once we're aloft conversation is difficult.'

Germain, who had probably flown as many miles as the young charter-pilot, explained the area he wanted to go over, exactly as he'd defined it the previous evening, but with an added instruction.

'Pine Butte, the mountain with a lake on the top of it . . . I'd like to see it, but not fly over it. If there is a road leading to it up some canyon, I'd like to reconnoitre that too. Okay?'

Jack Skinner leaned to try his starter. 'Okay,' he said, and for as long as it took him to get his motors running and warmed up, he sat in faintly-frowning thought.

It did not take them as long to get airborne as it took them to get clearance from the flight-tower to taxi forth for take-off. Afterwards, Skinner banked completely around the tower, then figured his course and set the aeroplane to it.

The morning aloft was even more exquisite than it had been down below. Far ahead, northeast, rose a gigantic mountain with snow-streamers down each of its seamy gullies, and also with what Germain assumed was a year-round patch of glacial ice across its high crown. Then Jack Skinner veered slightly northwest and his wingtip obscured Germain's vision. He meant to find out the name of that huge mountain, but ten minutes later he had forgotten all about it.

At mountaintop level it was an altogether different world. The peaks and rims were sun-splashed and bright, but midway down each slope the night gloom lingered, and would probably continue to do so in the deeper canyons, most of the morning, and after high-noon, would turn dark again for the balance of the day.

Some of the ranges were formidable. Once, they skimmed along on the north side of a glacial icefield that shone as smooth, and slick, as dirty glass. Another time, as Jack Skinner headed almost due west, it was possible to see an enormous cloud-field, as flat and level as a prairie, but all this was diaphanous, formed by the sea below which could not be seen.

Germain marvelled at this altogether unknown and unsuspected part of California. It was wild, unsettled, as primitive as anything in Montana or Wyoming, places usually thought to possess the last Western frontier.

Finally, Skinner flew due north for as long as was required to get over a rather large, hidden valley, then he turned and headed back on an angle which would take them above Scarpino's mountaintop, but as though they were simply flying a south-eastern pattern coming down from up north somewhere. Skinner explained none of this, but he handed Inspector Germain a map and traced their course with a finger.

Germain was pleased; he was also curious. Obviously his remark that he wanted to see the top of Scarpino's mountain had aroused some interest — or suspicion — in Jack Skinner. It was also obvious now, from the clever way Skinner was devising their over-flight, that he knew Germain was not just a sightseeing holidaymaker. Germain wondered what Jack Skinner really thought of him.

The sun was at their backs on the return trip, but high enough by ten o'clock to fill in most of the more shallow canyons. Hundreds of miles southward rose a grey-pale pall so immense and high that it was visible as far off as Germain was. Skinner leaned and said, 'San Francisco. If everyone could see what air pollution *really* is, from up here, they'd cry a lot louder.'

Germain nodded. He didn't give a tinker's damn about San Francisco's air-pollution problem. He was watching Scarpino's mountaintop come closer, down below. Skinner glanced down there, too, once in a while, but only to keep his route on the normal over-flight as though he were passing down from up north on a perfectly ordinary flight.

Germain saw the blue-water lake and marvelled at its beautiful colour. He saw the meadow that went completely around the lake, and for a moment as they passed over, he caught a glimpse of a rooftop that was very steep on some kind of an unusual-looking building down there. No one was on the lake and as far as he could determine as they sped past there was no one on the big meadow. Then they were past and Skinner dropped down a little and pointed. A dirt road snaked its way up a crooked canyon down the far, or southerly, slope of Scarpino's mountain. Germain gestured for Skinner to bank northward and trace the road back to where it junctured with some arterial throughway.

They accomplished that within minutes. There was a little town where the carriageway went arrow-straight north and south. That was where the canyon road branched off and went like a sick snake up between slopes and cliffs.

Germain had seen all he cared about so Jack Skinner nodded and sought altitude for the run back down to the bay area. There was beginning to be a mild heat haze as earth temperatures soared, and although it would not continue as far southward as San Francisco, the smog and fog down there looked the same, so most of the distance back to the airport they rode above a fine, mist-like vapour which did not reach to their height and therefore did not impair the diamond clarity of the upper atmosphere.

Skinner pointed towards the nearing sea. 'Beautiful,' he called, and Germain nodded. He was able, now, to appreciate the view without any other diversions, but he did not think, as his pilot seemed to think, that the sea was nearly as beautiful to look at as all those stairstepped mountains behind them, blue-blurry now as they sped down the valleys towards the most cosmopolitan of California cities.

There was the usual delay above San Francisco. Skinner was on his radio constantly for the last two hundred miles. He took time out, once, to complain to Germain of the intolerably crowded conditions at the airport. Otherwise he kept on the air.

They had to circle three times before being signalled to come down. Germain heard the crackling radio without paying much attention to it; that was his pilot's concern. He viewed the city, the Bay Bridge, even the old stone ruin off shore that had been the federal prison for incorrigibles a few years back — Alcatraz Island.

Then Skinner ran down his engines and made a long, very smooth and professional approach, touched down, and Allan Germain loosened his safety harness. The flight was finished. Germain had accomplished his purpose.

8

The Idea That Jelled

Sergeant Moore called in an officer from the intelligence unit named Berryman, Ronald Berryman. Moore did not appear to be very anxious above involvement with Inspector Germain's scheme. As he said, after Berryman had been filled in, his bureau operated within the city's limits and had nothing to do, even with the affairs of the country, let alone affairs of counties as far north as the one where Scarpino had his mountaintop.

Allan Germain's contention was that Angelo Scarpino had not sent for Joe Buono to kill some local rustic in the cow-country where his mountaintop was, he had sent for Buono because a much more important murder was imminent.

Sergeant Moore did not dispute this. He simply remained obdurate. 'Okay, maybe he's going to have this Joe Buono hit someone bigger, maybe even another Mafia bigwig, and you're right, inspector, in wanting to know who it's going to be. But whatever you do is strictly on your own. I may be able to help out within the city limits, but if you go up there to Angelo Scarpino's mountaintop, you will have to do it all as a private citizen, and from what I've heard about Scarpino, I wouldn't advise it.'

The man from Intelligence Unit said, 'There isn't any trouble within the local families, Mr Germain. There actually is never any trouble between families — well — if there is, it never gets to us, and as far as the police are concerned that's the same as no trouble. If they want to hit one another we're all to the good, aren't we? As for Angelo Scarpino . . . ' Berryman shook his head wanly. 'He doesn't even belong here. He's got no say around San Francisco. I know he's high in the Council. They may have got word to him to take out D'Angelo or someone else out here, but it's unusual. Normally, the Council would contact a local chieftain.'

'Suppose this is something private,' said Germain. 'Suppose the Council doesn't know about it.'

Berryman shrugged. 'It could be, of course, but if it is, Scarpino might tread on some sensitive toes. The local bosses wouldn't like having an outsider even from within the organization, come out here and get the heat turned on everyone by knocking someone off, even if it wasn't anyone within the organization.'

Germain did not yield. 'All right. Let's go back a moment; if the Council sent word to Scarpino to take someone out, the local bosses would be told of it, wouldn't they?'

Berryman nodded. 'In all probability, yes, but it would have to be someone pretty damned important for the council to have Scarpino, the *voyeur*, the outsider, order the hit in this area.'

'And suppose,' said Germain, 'Scarpino saw something out here he didn't like and told the Council back east.'

Berryman nodded again. 'Possible. If it was his initiative they'd probably delegate the solution to him. Also, Angelo

Scarpino isn't just a *capo*. He either has sat on the Council or has been damned close to sitting on it. In either case he's one of the bigshots.' Berryman looked at Sergeant Moore. 'It does look as though there might be something, Reg.'

Moore had never denied that and he did not deny it now. 'Sure there's something. All I'm saying, Ron, is that S.F.P.D. can't jump out of character. We are a city police force.' He shot a look at Allan Germain. 'Inspector, I don't mean to sound derogatory — but what in the hell do we actually have here? D'Angelo's confirmation of your suspicions? And what else? The arrival of an assassin to see Angelo Scarpino. It doesn't even have to mean Buono is going to hit someone; he could be carrying some important news to Scarpino. He could be visiting because he needs to be somewhere else for a while.'

Germain played his trump card. 'He's wanted on suspicion of murder in Chicago, Sergeant. That ought to be enough for you to lean on him.'

Moore nodded briskly. 'All right. You

tell me where to find him *within the city*, and believe me, Inspector, I'll lean on him hard. But this other stuff — this going up to some damned mountaintop off in the boondocks — is too far out for me.'

Berryman had an idea. 'Reg, it would be something if we could land someone like Scarpino.'

Moore was getting exasperated. 'How, damn it all? Angelo Scarpino's got some of the best criminal lawyers in the world representing him. I'd give a years' pay to nail someone as high in the Cosa Nostra as Scarpino, but if the Federal Government can't do it, how can we?'

'If Buono hits someone,' said Berryman, 'I think there's a fair chance we can tie Scarpino to it.' He looked at Germain. 'If Buono is up there, then he hired a car here in the city. You've traced him to San Francisco, Inspector, what needs to be done now is trace him right up to Scarpino's front door.'

Sergeant Moore listened and mulled this new tangent over for a few moments. Then he said, 'Okay, Inspector, we'll do that much; we'll find out where he rented his car, or who he hired to drive him up there. But after that, unless something more turns up, we can't put any more time on it. Is that agreeable with you?'

It had to be, obviously, so Germain nodded, but he was a lot less interested in how Joe Buono got to Scarpino's mountaintop than he was in who Buono was on the West Coast to kill.

That ended the meeting. It was late in the afternoon. Germain had had one of his usual busy days. If Sergeant Moore had known Germain's bureau chief back in Chicago, and if they had been able to talk together, Moore would have learned that Allan Germain was one of those tenacious people who not only never gave up, but who never took time off when he was working on something that held his interest.

Not that this was unusual, actually, but where Sergeant Moore had to dig in his heels was where Allan Germain, who was strictly on his own, could keep on going; he had much more latitude as a man on holiday than he would have had if he had been on an official assignment, while Moore was compelled by regulations to view everything he did or authorised others to do, strictly within the limitations of legality, and the Police Manual.

Germain went back to his hotel, showered, got comfortable, had a quart of pale ale sent up, stoked his pipe and went back in his mind's eye to the aerial view he'd had of Scarpino's hideaway.

An idea came like a blow from a bony fist.

He put aside his glass of beer and his pipe, went to the telephone and put in a call for Jack Skinner out at the charter-aeroplane compound of San Francisco Airport. It took time; Skinner was down the line with his aeroplane and someone had to be sent after him. While Germain waited he re-examined the idea, found it plausible, and had barely glanced at his wristwatch when Jack Skinner's voice came from the other end of the connection.

Germain identified himself. He asked if Skinner would be down at the airport for another hour or so, and when he was told that Skinner would be, Germain offered to buy him a steak dinner if he would wait until Germain could catch a cab and drive out. Skinner liked that suggestion, so Germain got dressed again, drank what beer remained in his glass, pocketed his cold pipe and went in search of a taxi.

It was almost eight o'clock but there was still daylight. The sun was gone, the moon would not arise for another half to three-quarters of an hour, and during the interim twilight as bright as mid-afternoon lingered, making the visibility excellent for Germain's driver as they sped out to the airport.

Skinner was waiting at the lower end of the cement ramp, when Germain went down it. Skinner smiled, but his eyes were both wary and curious. Germain asked where a good restaurant was and Skinner pointed back the way Germain had just come.

'Airport café, Mr Germain. It's not only the best, it's also the only restaurant close by.'

That is where they went, and Skinner was right. The food was excellent and despite the turmoil and confusion, the service was also good. Midway through their meal Jack Skinner gazed directly at Germain and said, 'You want to fly again tomorrow, is that it?'

That wasn't it. Germain tasted his coffee, found it far better than he had expected, and put the cup aside to explain. 'What I want to find out, and if you can help me do it I'll be glad to pay you, is whether or not anyone among the charter-pilots has flown anyone in to that mountaintop we flew over today.'

Skinner didn't even hesitate with his reply. 'Sure they have. Remember that guy who came by last night and told me I owed the drinks? Well, he owns that French helicopter down at the far end of the area, the big blue-and-white one. He had a contract most of the summer, probably paid off his chopper. He hauled in people, building materials, workmen, even a damned big electric generator.'

'People?'

'Yeah. In fact, the day before you showed up he took a guy in who arrived on some scheduled flight.'

Germain reached for the cup again but did not lift it. He felt like a man holding his breath or walking a tightrope. 'You didn't by any chance see that guy, did you?'

'Yeah, I saw him,' said Skinner, and cocked his head at Germain. 'In fact, after you left yesterday and I was heading for the tavern, that pilot nailed me. I told him what you wanted — to fly over a peak up north. This morning I kept wondering — his reaction was like I'd jabbed him with a pin.'

Germain forgot the coffee. 'And . . . ?'

'Nothing. He just acted like you had no business doing that. He didn't say any more but he was quiet and thoughtful the rest of the evening.'

Germain had a vision that disturbed him; he used Skinner to verify it. 'By any chance, did this pilot fly out last night or early this morning?'

Skinner shrugged. 'The chopper was gone when I showed up on the line. That would have been about six this morning.'

Germain softly said, 'Gawd damn.'

Skinner was interested. 'What's wrong?'

Germain evaded the question. 'What is the helicopter pilot's name?'

'Lloyd Harlan. What's wrong, Mr Germain?'

For a while Allan Germain sat and thought. *Now*, he recalled how the helicopter pilot had acted last night when he and Jack Skinner had come together down on the tarmac after Germain had hired Skinner, and had told him what he wanted.

It also troubled him to learn that the helicopter had been gone so early in the morning. He could guess where it had flown to without any trouble at all: Scarpino's mountaintop. He could also guess why it had flown there: Lloyd Harlan, because Scarpino had hired him most of the summer and had unquestionably paid Harlan very well, felt some kind of loyalty. Or else he was just money-hungry. In either case, he had flown up and had told Scarpino there was someone flying around trying to spy on the mountaintop.

'Blew it,' he said cheerfully, to the baffled man across the table. 'How well do you know Lloyd Harlan?'

'Well enough. You want me to find out where he went so damned early this morning, is that it?'

Germain fished forth a packet of notes, peeled off two and put them under Skinner's water glass. He then gave Skinner his suite number at the hotel as well as his telephone number, and finally finished his coffee before rising. 'Find out and telephone me at the hotel. How good an infiltrator can you be?'

Skinner picked up the two notes, examined them, smiled as he shoved them into a trouser pocket and said, 'You want me to ferret this information out of Lloyd without him getting suspicious, then telephone it to you, right?'

Germain smiled. 'Right as rain. No matter what time it is, call me.' He picked up the tab, left a fat tip for the waitress, and led the way to the cashier's booth where he paid, then he followed the younger man out of the terminal building into a settling, sooty kind of a night. There was a light wind coming in off the sea, it smelled noticeably of salt-spray.

Jack Skinner lit a cigarette and turned slowly to study Allan Germain. 'What am I getting into?' he asked.

Germain's answer was blunt. 'Nothing, if you get the information for me without him knowing it.'

'Okay, but who are you, and is Lloyd in trouble?'

'He's in no trouble at all, even if he did what I think he did this morning. But he could be in all kinds of trouble if he hangs on with the man who owns that mountaintop.' Germain did not answer the first part of Skinner's question. He simply smiled, nodded, and went hiking back up the ramp to the taxi stand. Behind him, Jack Skinner stood looking after him. Skinner's inner turmoil was natural. He had been asked to pry information from a friend and pass it along to a stranger. He might have decided not to do it after all, but the moment he shoved his hands into trouser pockets and went hiking towards the tavern where he was sure Lloyd Harlan would still be, he touched those large-denomination notes in his pocket.

It was too late to hand them back, Germain was gone. He didn't want to hand them back anyway. If he looked at it right, he really wasn't harming Lloyd any. With squared shoulders he hastened back to the tavern.

9

Some Optional Victims

The call came later, but Germain was a light sleeper and he was unconsciously awaiting it. Skinner said, 'Yeah, Lloyd flew to Pine Mountain this morning.'

Germain had his answer. But Jack Skinner had more to say.

'Yesterday he brought some guy back out of there. The same guy he flew in the day before. The guy who arrived on one of the scheduled runs. His name was Harrison.'

Germain said, 'Very good — unless you got Harlan to wondering.'

Skinner was confident on that score. 'No, I don't think so. We sat and exchanged stories about you and this other guy. Our most recent charters. Lloyd was interested in you. I made out like you were some kind of government official making a forestry survey. Lloyd

109

said he thought you were some kind of a cop, and he told me who that man is on the mountaintop, Angelo Scarpino, the bigtime hoodlum.'

'And that's probably what your friend told Scarpino,' said Germain. 'That a cop was flying over his hideout yesterday.'

Skinner hung fire a moment. 'Well, maybe, but he didn't say so.'

Germain ended the conversation, rang off, got up from bed and walked to the window that faced northward towards the invisible faraway mountains. Scarpino knew someone was interested in his mountaintop, meaning him, and that was all it would take for him to pull all the stops to be on guard. Driving up that hidden canyon road was out. If Scarpino had anyone up there with him at all, they'd perch on a rim of the mountaintop and see the dust from a car coming an hour before the car even got close.

Scarpino wasn't that important to Germain at the moment anyway. If Harlan had brought Joe Buono back to the city it would be for one of two reasons, to buy passage on an outgoing airliner, or to kill someone in San Francisco.

If Buono had bought passage out of the city, by now he was long gone. Harlan had brought him out of the mountains yesterday. If he was still in the city, he would be setting up an assassination.

One way, the element of time wasn't important. The other way, if he was to kill someone, the element of time was *very* important.

Germain glanced at his watch, found that it was not quite midnight, and telephoned Moore's bureau for his residential telephone number. Then he got Sergeant Moore out of bed to tell him what he now knew.

Moore didn't sound very drowsy, so perhaps he hadn't been in bed very long, but he *did* sound both exasperated and resigned. 'I'll send a team to the airport tonight and see if they can turn up anything. It would help like hell if we knew which name he was using this time.'

'Try them all,' said Germain, 'including his own. I've got a photograph; perhaps I ought to take it down there right now.'

Moore said, very drily, 'Never mind. I also have photographs of Joe Buono. I had them wired in yesterday. The officers can use my copies. And if he didn't fly out . . . ?'

'He's in the city to hit someone,' said Germain, thinking Moore had to be sleepy whether he sounded it or not, to ask a question with such an obvious answer.

'It's a very big city, Inspector Germain. Even if the night-duty-officer will have a couple of teams up for an assignment, I don't think we'll turn up anything tonight. Maybe not for a couple of days, in fact. San Francisco has more bedrooms than any city I've ever heard of.'

'But you'll put the teams out,' said Germain, 'won't you? If he's here, you can bet money he's not after D'Angelo, Sergeant. And you heard what Berryman said; it's not very likely he's going to hit some other Cosa Nostra bigwig. What does that leave?'

'Tell me,' said Sergeant Moore, 'I'm fascinated.'

Germain grinned because the sarcasm

didn't bother him in the least, he was accustomed to it from every Reginald Moore type he'd ever met. 'How about your mayor, Sergeant? How about Ronald Reagan? What foreign diplomats are currently visiting San Francisco? How the hell do I know who he's going to hit — but I'll still bet good money that if he's successful there's going to be one hell of a scandal around here.'

Moore seemed to come slightly to life. 'Come by my office in the morning, Inspector, maybe we'll have something.'

Germain put down the telephone, went to stand another few moments at the window, then he went reluctantly back to bed with one consoling thought: Joe Buono was probably also in bed.

Morning came early for Germain, as it customarily did. He had breakfast at an uptown restaurant because the hotel's dining-room didn't even open until nine o'clock, then he took his time walking the short distance to Moore's office.

Moore was already there, and Ronald Berryman of the intelligence unit was also there. Berryman was smoking but Moore was not. When Germain walked in both men looked at him and nodded. Moore held up some stapled sheets of paper. 'Photostatic copies of passenger lists from the airport. No one named Harrison, Bennington, Carlysle, or Joe Buono left the city on a scheduled flight yesterday.' Moore dropped the lists and leaned on the desk. 'Just how good is your source of information on Buono, Inspector? I meant to ask you that last night, and forgot.'

Germain related all he had learned from Jack Skinner, and Sergeant Moore leaned back at his desk. 'Okay, now we're getting somewhere. I'll have this chopper pilot picked up and brought in for questioning.' His large palm hovered above some buttons on the edge of the desk. 'Unless you've got a better idea?'

Germain smiled blandly. 'That was what I would have suggested, Sergeant.'

The big hand descended upon one particular button, then Sergeant Moore reached for his telephone and held it to his face as Ronald Berryman stubbed out his cigarette and looked at

Inspector Germain.

'I've been doing some groundwork on this affair, Inspector. I don't know how you've arrived at your conclusions but they shape up fairly well. We got some F.B.I info on this Joseph Buono yesterday. He's considered one of the deadliest Mafia killers still alive. He has been Angelo Scarpino's favourite for quite a few years. We didn't get the complete dossier but we got enough.'

Moore finished talking over the telephone and put this instrument back upon its cradle with a thoughtful look. 'They'll bring the chopper pilot to my office, providing he's on the ground.' Sergeant Moore seemed to show more concern now than he had shown before. He tossed the airline passenger list copies into a mail basket and considered Allan Germain rather sombrely. 'You've been sleeping with this thing, Inspector,' he said. 'What's your guess about Buono's target?'

Germain had no answer. He'd tried to come up with one for his own edification upon several occasions and had failed.

'For one thing,' he explained to Moore, 'we don't know *why* someone should be hit. Mr Berryman said there is no rumble from within any of the local families. Even the *capo* who has income-tax problems, isn't a likely prospect.'

Moore wasn't interested in the Cosa Nostra people. 'As long as they'll stick to killing each other, Inspector, I'll even chip in to help buy the bullets. That's not what's sticking in my mind right at the moment. Let me put it another way: If it's *not* some member of a local Mafia family, who might it be?'

Germain still had no answer. 'It's your city, Sergeant. All I'm willing to gamble on is that it's someone big, and it's someone who is able to make serious trouble for either Scarpino or the Cosa Nostra establishment.'

Ronald Berryman jerked straight up in his chair. 'Why didn't you think of him before?' he exclaimed, staring at Reginald Moore.

'Think of who?' demanded the sergeant.

'Hale Buchanan, Reg. Who else?'

116

Moore and Berryman sat gazing at one another until Moore turned very slowly and said, 'The City Attorney, Inspector Germain. He's got a thing about the Cosa Nostra. He's the guy who's been bleeding D'Angelo about how the organization works; names, positions, all that stuff.'

Germain took his time. He fished forth his smokes, lit one and considered the window in the rear wall of Moore's office. It wasn't Carmine D'Angelo, he was positive of that, and Berryman had convinced him it probably wasn't another Cosa Nostra chieftain. But it was someone worth importing one of the best assassins in the business to kill. A City Attorney would fit very well. If the City Attorney was someone who was gathering evidence against the Mafia, someone who had got hold of a valid informer and was draining him dry in exchange for drugs and protection, that kind of a City Attorney would fit *very* well.'

'Hit him,' said Germain, 'so that no one else would dare use the information he's acquired. Or maybe they want him killed so they can get his Cosa Nostra files.' Germain looked over at Berryman. 'You've come up with the best target yet.'

Moore lunged for his telephone, dialled, spoke briefly, then put the telephone aside again and said, 'We just got a small break. Mr Buchanan is still down in Sacramento. He was supposed to return this afternoon, but his office just told me he wouldn't be back until probably late tomorrow night. We just got a reprieve.'

Germain wasn't very impressed. 'You said a little while ago it would take a lot of digging to find Buono in your city. Can you do it before tomorrow night?'

Moore was honest. 'I don't know. I doubt it like all hell.'

Berryman didn't add any encouragement. 'Reg, this Buono is one of their best.'

'Damn it, I am aware of that!'

'Let me finish,' exclaimed Berryman. 'He will have all day tomorrow to find out that Mr Buchanan isn't expected back until tomorrow night. The question is: Will he know Hale Buchanan by sight, by then, or will he lie over an extra day, and take a position outside the Court House and when Mr Buchanan drives up — bingo!?'

Germain answered ahead of Sergeant Moore. 'I'll opt for tomorrow night. Buono won't need any more time to arrange to leave the city than one day. He can be already on his way when he takes up a position on one of the upper-deck ramps at the airport to keep an eye on incoming flights. That's damned well lighted all around, out there — except on those ramps. He'll have a perfect sighting as this City Attorney of yours alights and strolls into the terminal. He can nail him with his silencer — take my word for it, he uses one — and be on board his own flight out of San Francisco before anyone gets a hunt organized. For Buono, it's an ideal set-up.'

Moore's sarcasm came up again. 'An ideal set-up sure as hell.' He rose behind the desk. 'Excuse me for a little while. I'm going to see if the captain will detail more men to the search for this legendary assassin. If Buono's got today and tomorrow, so have *we*.' He left the office

119

with a brisk step.

Ronald Berryman lit another cigarette, considered the tip carefully, and finally smiled. 'Suppose we've guessed wrong, Inspector?'

The answer was obvious. 'Well, in that case Mr Berryman, you'll have a perfectly healthy City Attorney day after tomorrow — and your city coroner will have a corpse, won't he? How does a police force cover all the people a Cosa Nostra killer might have a contract on?'

Berryman was not discouraged. 'It could be done. I even believe our Commissioner of Police might go for it. Where would we start, at all the local embassies, maybe, and all the nightspots operated by shady characters? Or at the offices and residences of all the city and county state officials?'

'Not the embassies,' replied Germain. 'Those people aren't liable to be involved with Mafia chieftains.'

Berryman's eyes twinkled sardonically. 'I wish I could tell you some of what we know about Mafia people and a few local embassy people. But you're right; the odds are damned high against that kind of a killing.' Berryman put out his half-smoked cigarette and stood up. 'I hope you'll excuse me too, Inspector. I think Intelligence Unit might want a piece of this action. We've also got some people we'd like to protect.'

Germain was left alone. He rose and strolled around the office killing time until Sergeant Moore returned. He read the names of the law books on the shelves, read the names and dates of the Police Bureau publications that were also neatly shelved, and was impressed at how seriously Sergeant Moore took his profession.

Finally, Germain stopped in front of a large window and looked towards San Francisco Bay over the multicoloured rooftops of the city, and told himself that if Joe Buono didn't make some attempt to kill an important person, forever after when a Californian assignment cropped up in his Chicago precinct, the best thing Allan Germain could do was be terribly busy on something that would prevent him from being assigned.

10

A Killer Is Loose

Before the helicopter pilot, Lloyd Harlan, was brought to Sergeant Moore's office, and shortly after the departure of Ronald Berryman, Moore returned with a handsome, grey, professional-looking man who might have been a successful doctor or lawyer, and introduced him to Germain as Captain Russell Beaman, chief of homicide bureau.

Germain was very impressed. His own bureau chief back in Chicago was a lot less presentable in appearance, although he probably did not have to yield much to Russell Beaman in either intelligence or police expertise.

The captain asked Germain to be seated, then he asked to have Germain's story from the very beginning. As Germain complied, and watched Captain Beaman's face, he got the feeling that

Beaman was probably as much a politician as he was a bureau chief. But he also thought that Beaman was assessing both Germain and his story from the standpoint of a man who would have to make the decisions, and that whatever else Captain Beaman was, he was not afraid of involvement. At least that was what Germain hoped would prove to be the case.

When Germain had told it all as bluntly as he knew how Captain Beaman smiled very affably and looked at Sergeant Moore. 'Reg, we've gone for weeks at a time on one hell of a lot less evidence.'

Moore agreed. 'Yes, sir, but what we're going to have to do now is practically strip the bureau, and maybe even borrow men, to try and find this Joe Buono in the city, before he makes his attempt on the City Attorney — *if* he makes it.'

Captain Beaman proved himself a little out of touch by saying, 'Why don't we just stake out the airport — blanket it — and nail him before he can do anything?'

Moore's answer was short. 'Because, Captain, if it's *not* the City Attorney, and it hits the newspapers that we were covering the wrong man while the real victim was shot to death without a chance, it's going to make things pretty damned hot for us for a while. I think what we've got to do is find Joe Buono before he gets into position. That's why I went up to your office; to get your approval to make a real effort to find Buono no later than tomorrow morning.'

Beaman drifted his gaze back to Germain. 'Inspector, any ideas?'

Germain had one but he did not think this was the time to propose it. The last thing he wanted to do was make Sergeant Moore look bad in front of his precinct superior. 'I think the sergeant is perfectly right, sir,' he said. 'It would be a lot better, time and trouble wise, to nail Buono before he makes his assassination-try.'

Beaman rose. 'Sergeant, I'll call around and see which men can be re-assigned.' He left the office and Sergeant Moore sat gazing at Germain.

'What was your idea, Inspector?'

Germain raised Moore one notch in his personal opinion. 'Send someone down to Sacramento either to bodyguard the City Attorney down there, and talk him into staying away until you can find Buono, or, if he can't keep him down there, ride back with him on the night-flight — both of them fitted with flak-vests.'

Moore smiled. 'Except for the flak-vests, I've already talked to Berryman down in his office. I had to wait a few minutes to see the captain. Berryman himself is going down. Anything else?'

If Germain had another suggestion he got no chance to explain it; one big set of knuckles rolled over the door, then it opened and a pleasant-faced big burly plainclothesman ushered Lloyd Harlan into Moore's office. The pleasant-faced man said, 'No problems, Sergeant. Do you need me any more?'

The sergeant shook his head while he ran a seasoned glance up and down Lloyd Harlan. 'No. Thank you.' As the door closed Sergeant Moore motioned Harlan to a chair, which the pilot took without paying as much attention to the sergeant as he paid to Allan Germain. Harlan did not appear truculent, but he seemed suspicious and very wary. When Moore asked about his charter licence he demonstrated a knowledge of charter-flyers Germain did not have. Instantly, Lloyd Harlan was defensive. Evidently for the police to get a charter-licence revoked was not very difficult, and just as obvious to Germain, was Harlan's dread of having this happen.

Moore then demonstrated another facet of knowledge Germain did not possess. He asked if Harlan had filed copies of all his flights with the city airport authority as well as with the Civil Aeronautics Authority, Harlan said that he had, and that if Moore wished, he would bring in his copies.

Moore didn't press this issue; all he'd wanted was to draw Harlan out, to get him accustomed to talking. Next, Moore said, 'Who have you been doing most of your charter work for this summer?'

Harlan swivelled a look at Germain before answering. 'Well, for a guy who bought the top of a mountain several hundred miles north.'

'What's his name?'

Harlan winced. 'Angelo Scarpino.'

'The big-time criminal?' asked Moore, looking stony.

Harlan nodded. 'Yeah, I suppose it's the same one. But when a guy named Mario first contacted me early this last spring to fly in building materials, I had no idea who the big man was. I didn't really know his name until I'd hauled in some parts of pre-fabricated A-frame, and a lot of other stuff like an electrical generator and a motorboat.' Harlan looked at Germain again, and shrugged thick shoulders.

'Of course I've read about Scarpino in the newspapers — who hasn't? But he never asked me to do anything like fly in dope or anything like that. I was just his work-horse when he was fixing up that mountaintop.'

Germain spoke for the first time. 'Yesterday morning, Lloyd . . . why did you fly to see Scarpino?'

Harlan's expression underwent a subtle

change. He looked from Germain to Moore, then on past to the rear-wall window. 'You know why I went in there yesterday, Mr Germain. To tell him a friend of mine, another charter-pilot, had agreed to take some guy over Pine Butte, who looked like a cop to me.' Harlan's gaze went back to Germain and clung there. 'And I was right, wasn't I, you are a cop?'

Germain didn't answer. 'Who was up there with Scarpino?'

'His wife,' answered Harlan. 'Himself, and that guy named Mario. And a guy named Benny. That's all.'

'But there was a fifth one,' prompted Germain.

'Mr Harrison, sure. But I brought him out day before yesterday.'

Sergeant Moore pounced, because this was the crux of the entire conversation as far as he was concerned. 'Where did you leave Mr Harrison, Harlan?'

'At the airport. He had an overnight case with him. The same one he had with him when I picked him up three days ago and took him to Mr

Scarpino's summer place.'

'Did Harrison book a flight out, do you know?' asked Moore.

Harlan looked annoyed. 'I wouldn't know that. He didn't say anything from the time he got in until we landed. The same as when I first flew him in a few days ago. Not a lousy word.' Harlan paused, then brightened. 'Well, *he* didn't say anything, but when Mario was seeing him off out in the meadow beside my chopper, Mario said something like — 'remember what he said, come back any time for the fishing.' I thought at the time I'd probably get another fare for bringing Harrison back . . . Is Harrison really his name?'

Neither Moore nor Germain answered Harlan's question. 'What do you know about Mr Harrison?' asked Sergeant Moore. 'What has anyone said to you about him, anyone at all?'

Harlan looked Moore in the eye when he answered. 'I don't know anything about him. He was just some dude all dressed up in fancy clothes, when I first flew him in, and like I've already told you, he didn't say two words going in or coming back out.'

Germain shot a question. 'How much did Scarpino pay you for telling him you thought a cop was spying on him from the air?'

Lloyd Harlan showed a faint stain of colour. 'Three hundred dollars. And in case you're thinking I'm some kind of a fink, let me tell you something; Mr Scarpino paid me darned well to ferry in his building material this summer. I've darn near cleared off my chopper. Anyone who treats a man as well as I was treated deserves something back. Maybe you don't think so, Mister, but I do.'

Germain let that harangue go past. 'When are you to go in again?'

'Later on today. I'm to take in a big list of groceries and sundry items, and when I come back out Mario is to ride back with me. No one said, but I got the impression that Mario has business down here in San Francisco. That'll leave just Mr and Mrs Scarpino up there, and Benny.' At the blank look he got, Harlan said, 'Benny is Mr Scarpino's sort of straw boss up there.

He keeps out of sight though. The man you meet when you fly in is this Mario.'

Sergeant Moore rose and leaned on his desk. 'Lloyd,' he said quietly, 'you pose a real problem. I'd have to fake a charge to lock you up, but on the other hand a man who ran once to tell Scarpino someone was interested in him, up there, certainly would do the same thing again.'

Harlan had his own answer to that. 'Look; the last thing I want is trouble with the law. I owed that favour to Mr Scarpino, so I paid it. Otherwise, if there's some kind of serious trouble, I'll be glad to take a flight down the coast for a week or two.'

Moore was relentless. 'What good would a flight down the coast do? You could still wire back up here and have some other charter-pilot pass along the word.'

Lloyd Harland reacted about as Allan Germain thought he might. 'Look, Sergeant, I'm not a criminal. As far as I know I've broken no law. The only thing I've done in my dealings with Scarpino was go and tell him someone was interested enough in him to hire a friend of mine to fly them over his summer place. Okay, maybe most guys would have just minded their own business and kept out. Me, I happened to think I owed him that much. But that's all. As far as I'm concerned, from now on he can find himself another chopper.'

Sergeant Moore sat stoically behind his desk throughout all this. When the tirade ended he said, 'How far down the coast did you have in mind going, Mr Harlan?'

The tow-headed man thought a moment. 'Quite a ways, Sergeant. I've got an aunt and uncle down by Santa Barbara.'

Moore smiled. 'Have a nice trip, Mr Harlan.' He rose, still smiling. 'You can go if you'd like.' Moore let Harlan get to the door before he said, 'Don't doublecross us, will you, Mr Harlan?'

Instead of an answer, Moore got a glare that raked over Allan Germain as well, then Lloyd Harlan closed the door after himself. Moore said, 'Well, temporarily, Scarpino and his cliff-dwellers are stranded.'

Germain nodded without comment. The idea was novel and had not occurred to him until Moore made that remark. Of course Scarpino wasn't really stranded; there was the road below his mountain-top, and doubtless he had at least one car up there, and probably a jeep as well. Germain had seen no road going all the way up to the mountaintop but that did not preclude the possibility of there being one. Flying over rugged terrain that was heavily forested was not the best way to make a minute study of the landscape.

But road or no road, Germain was much less interested in Angelo Scarpino now that Joe Buono was in the city, than he had been before. Sergeant Moore's interest in Scarpino had never been particularly active even though Berryman of Intelligence had spoken a bit glowingly of the honours sure to accrue if S.F.P.D. could nail him.

Moore's interest was Joe Buono. As he said, when he leaned in his chair behind the desk and gazed dispassionately at Germain, 'I'd feel a hell of a lot better if this Joe Buono was a local figure.'

Germain continued silent. During the latter part of the interlude with Lloyd Harlan he had been considering things from Scarpino's viewpoint. It never paid to underestimate an enemy, and Angelo Scarpino did not have to know for a certainty that a policeman was actively interested in his mountaintop. All he had to do was *suspect* the police were getting aggressive, to become wary. He would assume that the police had something to back up their activity; Scarpino had been playing hide-and-seek with the police for many years. He would understand the rules of the game. Also, he would figure out that if the police *were* active, now might be a very poor time to have a Cosa Nostra gunman assassinate someone.

He might even go farther in his speculations and link the police activity with the arrival of Joe Buono. If he did that, and if he had already decided now was not the time for an assassination, he would probably contact Buono and call him off.

Without Harlan's helicopter, and probably unwilling to waste a lot of time locating another charter-chopper, it seemed to Germain that Scarpino's alternate course would be to send someone down to San Francisco by car. Without a telephone up there on Pine Butte, Scarpino's only routes of communication with the outside world were by air and by road.

Germain glanced at his watch, unwound up out of the chair and said, 'Sergeant; where is the nearest car-rental agency?'

Moore surprised Germain. 'Why bother?' Moore reached into a pocket, tossed over a pair of car keys. 'Take mine, it's parked out back in the slot with my name on it. What are you going to do?'

'*Maybe* I'm going to be able to pick up someone Scarpino will send down here by car to warn Buono the cops are stirred up.'

'And if he's already sent someone?'

Germain grinned. 'There's a little town at the junction of Scarpino's canyon road and the highway. If I know small towns, there'll be some nosy rustic up there who will have noticed if an outlander came out within the past ten hours or so.'

Sergeant Moore was agreeable. 'Possibly, Inspector, possibly.' He stood up from the desk. 'Get a description of the car and radio it to me. But if you pick up someone, tail him until you're sure he's coming down here, then use the radio, and we'll plan an interception. If he uses the normal carriageway we can take him when he has to slow down to cross the Bay Bridge.' Moore's broad brow furrowed a little. 'If it works it may save us one hell of a lot of time and effort in finding Buono.'

11

Into The Highlands

The reason Germain thought it would work was something Lloyd Harlan had said. He was supposed to fly in, pick up Mario, and bring him down to the city after unloading supplies. Lloyd had thought Mario had business in the city.

Germain could imagine what the business was — tell Joe Buono things were too hot for an assassination right at the moment.

Well, Harlan's chopper was not going to ferry in the supplies nor bring Mario off the mountaintop. He probably could have done it. The idea had crossed Germain's mind back at Moore's office. The reason he hadn't mentioned it was simply because Harlan had already proved that he felt some kind of loyalty towards Scarpino. Under just a little pressure, Harlan would have told all he knew, and by now Angelo Scarpino was sufficiently alert and suspicious to put on the pressure.

What Scarpino would think and how he would react by nightfall, when the blue-and-white helicopter had not arrived, was anyone's guess. Germain, who did not know the man personally, could only estimate Scarpino's reaction in relation to how he, himself, would react in Scarpino's shoes.

He had thought like that back in Sergeant Moore's office; Scarpino would be more anxious than ever to get word to Joe Buono. Also, in Scarpino's shoes, Allan Germain thought he would want to know what was happening. He would want Mario to ferret that out too, if he could.

Germain stoked up his pipe and drove through the late day with a roadmap on the seat beside him, but he didn't have to consult it yet; there were still a hundred and more miles of due-north driving ahead of him before he had to be concerned with locating the crossroads-village.

He was anxious about just one thing; if for some reason he and Sergeant Moore had overlooked, Mario was already on his way to the city by car, then Germain's long trip was all for nothing. Otherwise, there was the matter of timing. He thought that if the helicopter was not due until shortly before dark, he had a good chance of intercepting Mario. If the people on Scarpino's mountain were inclined to be lenient about the helicopter's schedule, then Germain's chances were still better.

Otherwise, Germain was satisfied that he had stolen a march on the Angelo Scarpino faction. Also, the City Attorney was out of Buono's reach, at least temporarily. If he were a reasonable man at all, and it was logical to assume that he was, he would not attempt to return to the city until he had either telephoned Sergeant Moore, or until Moore had contacted him through Berryman, to say all precautionary measures had been taken.

Perhaps the scales had swung just a little in favour of Inspector Germain, and his resigned associate, the San Francisco Police Department.

Germain met nightfall on an empty stomach but he did not take the time to stop and eat because he estimated that another hour and a half of driving would put him in the little village that was his destination. He was certain there would be a restaurant there, probably not a very elegant one, and probably nothing that would delight the cockles of a gourmet's heart, but then Germain was not a gourmet.

He was correct. The restaurant, when he finally reached the village, was plain to the point of nakedness and the food was mostly fried meat of one kind or another, but the greying, rather sharp-featured waitress — who was also the proprietress — was a veritable well-spring of local history, information, and titillating gossip. Her name, she told Germain, was Nanette Funk. She also informed him that she usually closed her café at six o'clock but that this evening the local school trustees were meeting across the road, something they did once a month,

140

and afterwards they traditionally trooped across the road and had pie and coffee. She was, by implication anyway, motivated strictly by a lofty dedication to duty and charitable service to those who served the small community.

Germain was hungry enough to actually enjoy deep-fat-fried hamburger, crisp onion rings, and coffee as black as original sin and almost as old, if taste was any indication. He was also willing to register genuine sympathy when Nanette Funk confided that she was a widow. Her late husband, Mortimer, had been killed in a logging accident several years earlier somewhere back in the westerly mountains. She was, by candid admission, only forty-six, strong as a horse and owned her café clear and unencumbered, and was also open to marital suggestions, but only because she liked having a man around to look after and fuss over.

Germain eased his way gingerly around this yawning abyss by bringing up the topic of eligible strangers as opposed to local yokels, and that was the key to what Widow Funk said next.

'Well, sir, would you believe it — one of the most notorious gangsters alive today, lives only eight miles back up the road west of town?'

Germain's astonishment was vast. 'No. Who is he?'

Mrs Funk looked left, then looked right, and ducked below her counter to reappear in a moment with a dogeared copy of a San Francisco newspaper with Angelo Scarpino's picture on an inside page, along with a discreet article mentioning that he had purchased land up north, and also gingerly handling a lot of old quotations from other, earlier, publications about his past, his Mafia affiliations, and his reputed great wealth.

Germain read the article, studied the heavy-jowled-face, and sipped a second cup of black coffee while Mrs Funk confided that although she had not seen Mr Scarpino personally, some of the local lumbermen had, when they had been up near his mountaintop cruising timber. Germain had no idea what 'cruising timber' was, and did not especially care.

'Doesn't he come down here to the

village? Doesn't he have people working for him who come down?'

Mrs Funk nodded. 'Yes. He's got two men up there. One of them, a squatty, greying man, runs errands hereabouts now and then, but they don't patronize my café nor Mr Gordon's grocery emporium across the road. We think all their supplies are flown in. There's a big blue-and-white helicopter that's been going in and out all summer, up there. That must be how they get their supplies.'

'This squatty man who comes out occasionally, what's his name?'

Mrs Funk did not know. 'Can't say as I've ever heard it. He don't seem to say a whole lot. Mr Gordon, who runs the store across the road and has the fourth-class postal office, told me none of those people up there get any mail.'

Germain finished his coffee, waved off a third cup and pointed to a woeful piece of chocolate pie inside a glass case which Mrs Funk brought to him as she shoved the other plates to one side.

'It's sort of mysterious,' she confided, as Germain worried off a piece of tough pie with his fork. 'Mostly, folks get to know something about one another around here, but those gangsters up there,' she shook here head. 'There's a rumour that they counterfeit money up there, a million dollars at a crack. We telephoned over to the County Seat and told the sheriff what we thought on that.'

'What did he say?'

Mrs Funk made a grimace. 'He's too busy playing F.B.I. agent and courthouse politics to come down and make a real investigation. They say that the big helicopter flies out that counterfeit money by the bushel-basket load.'

Germain couldn't finish the pie. It was tougher than he was. He bought a packet of cigarettes for which he had no particular use, then counted out enough silver to cover his meal, and slipped a generous tip under the lip of his coffee saucer. Mrs Funk's tawny, ferret eyes picked that up at once. She beamed up on Germain. 'If you weren't driving on through tonight,' she said, 'I've got cottages out back for rent to overnighters.'

Germain faced this unexpected largesse with a smile, drew forth money and offered to pay in advance for one of the cottages; after all, it would look a lot more legitimate if he had at least this poor excuse for lingering, watching for a car to arrive down the canyon road, in a town where the people seemed either not to sleep at all, or to sleep with one eye open in order to daily augment their interest in everything that happened.

Mrs Funk personally escorted Germain out through the weak light of kitchen windows to show him the cottage. It was one very plain room with three very plain windows, a large bed, a chair, and a steel pole with clothes hangers swaying from the down-canyon evening breeze that hadn't yet died away although Mrs Funk assured Germain that it would do so within a short while.

After she departed back to the café, Germain brought Moore's car round, parked it facing outward towards the canyon road, stoked up his pipe and strolled, hands in trouser pockets, back towards the dark canyon beyond the last house.

Generally the village lay on both sides of the highway, strung out north and south facing the roadway. Back where Germain strolled in the warm summer night, there were a few dilapidated vestiges of an earlier day when the village hadn't been so fawningly dependent upon the highway: old barns, some star-shaped old two-storey houses with broken windows and sagging rooflines, rotting corrals for horses and cattle, and an occasional skeletal steel windmill frame.

Beyond these mementoes of a more rugged era, lay the canyon road, unpaved, smelling strongly of hot earth and flour-fine tan dust, visible because it was much lighter than the flaring mountainsides on either side of it, pitching and turning as it followed an ancient creekbed-course.

Germain did not speculate on how old the road was or what kind of horse, mule, and even oxen, loads had come down out of its densely forested farthest reaches.

He was neither a romanticist nor a history buff. He stood in the shade of a roughly-made mortarstone building that had once housed a flourishing farrier's business, and listened.

The only sound of car traffic came from back towards the throughway where an occasional traveller cruised right on through heading north or south, as though the village did not exist, which it palpably didn't for most travellers; just enough stopped to keep it feebly alive.

The night had a scent Germain was not familiar with, it was compounded of sage sap, dust, hot rock, pine-scent and chaparral blossoms. It was spicy and, Germain thought, rather pleasant in a tawny way. At least it was preferable to city air and city odours.

He smoked his pipe, waited patiently to hear a car coming, did not hear one for as long as he stood out there, and finally turned to stroll back towards the front of town, where the highway passed through. If he had to be bored to death waiting, he might as well do it where there would be something more to view than just endless miles of dark and stark-standing, forested nothing.

It was entirely possible, although Germain chose not to believe it, that Scarpino's anxiety would not come to a head until dawn or thereafter, and that he might not dispatch Mario or Benny down the road until daylight returned.

If that were so, Germain told himself placidly as he walked along towards the lighted buildings along the highway, then he was going to have to keep an all-night vigil. It didn't particularly appeal to him, but then, neither had that horrible chocolate pie, but he'd overcome that, so he could do the same about an all-night watch.

12

Pursue And Intercept!

While he waited, Germain saw a black-and-white county sheriff's car cruise through, heading northward. Otherwise, as time passed, traffic dwindled to little else than an occasional huge truck-tractor. Also, the village's lights began to wink out here and there. It wasn't late, but in an area where boredom was never distant even in daylight, nightfall drove people to summertime television re-runs as soon as darkness fell, and from there, *really* bored, off to bed and sleep.

There was a telephone kiosk across the road in front of the general store. Germain considered telephoning Moore and decided against it because he could not remember the sergeant's residence-number, and also because whatever he might learn from Moore, it would not in all probability make any difference in what Germain had to do, which was wait.

It had been a long drive up to the village from the city. It had also been a rather long day for Germain. He had realized how tired he was when he'd viewed that ugly bed in the cottage he'd rented from Mrs Funk with appreciation.

Keeping the pipe going was a fair substitute for walking briskly but along towards midnight he walked too. It was possible to think of a number of reasons why Scarpino's man would not come driving down the dusty canyon-road so late at night. It was also possible to imagine two valid reasons why he *would* come down it; one reason was because by midnight Scarpino knew the helicopter was not coming, and two, because by midnight Scarpino would be on tenter-hooks to know just what exactly was going on.

The valid reasons won out. A little past one o'clock in the morning with a light chill settling into all the lower areas, and while Allan Germain was probably the only person still out of bed throughout the village, the car came.

But Germain did not hear it. Not at once, anyway. The way he knew a car was approaching was by the occasional flash of light ranging high across mountain-sides as the vehicle dipped down into a gully, then heaved upwards on the far side, headlamps tilted.

Germain's weariness did not drop away but his interest quickened sufficiently to drive him over to Moore's car where he climbed in behind the steering-wheel and sat, waiting and watching. All around him, except for lamps overhead at both ends of the village where the highway passed through, the town was dark and hushed. Even so, he could not quite detect the sound of the car coming down out of the dark canyon until he had visual contact with the headlamps, and then it was possible to hear the car only because, as the canyon narrowed somewhat before widening again behind the village, the acoustics threw sound ahead.

Germain's problem was elemental; as far has he knew there was no one else back up that canyon, but this was the holiday time of year and campers were everywhere. Of course, if the car stopped at the village and went no further, or if it turned right, or northward, then Germain did not have to be concerned. If it turned southward towards the city there was still an even chance it wasn't someone from the Scarpino place, but if it *did* turn southward, he was going after it.

When the vehicle was visible as it slowed to cruise past Germain sitting in the darkness of Sergeant Moore's car, before entering the village, it was close enough for Germain to see it quite well. It was a dark brown, heavy Lincoln Continental Mark Three. Germain smiled to himself. No holiday maker he had ever seen, went camping in a fifteen-thousand-dollar car. He let the Continental go past, out of sight into the village, then switched on Moore's vehicle and eased quietly ahead.

On ahead, the Continental's brilliant red rear lamps flashed as the driver braked to a halt at the two-way junction. Germain hung back, lights out, almost holding his breath. Then the Continental turned southward and Germain said,

'Amen!' and eased forward with his lights out until he too had reached the intersecting junction. The Continental was already far down the highway. Germain had his first misgivings as he turned on to the highway, cruised halfway through the village before switching on his headlamps, and pressed down on the accelerator.

Sergeant Moore's car was a good one, in the medium-priced field. Its manufacturers had never made any claim that it could keep pace with a Continental Mark Three. Few cars on the road could do that, including that other heavy competitor for the high-priced trade, the Cadillac.

Germain had a two-way transceiver set with which he could signal ahead at any time, but if he used it before reaching the San Francisco area he would have California Highway Patrol cars boiling out like hornets to make an interception, which was precisely what he did not want.

He drove Moore's car to the brink of rashness and held it there mile after mile. The car responded well, but it felt perilously close to soaring into the air each time it came up out of a dip in the roadway. The Continental up ahead did not increase the lead, as it probably would have, and definitely could have, if its driver had known he was being pursued. The distance was greater than it normally would have been, but not by Germain's choice.

Two factors contributed to this situation. One of course was the Continental itself, a masterfully built car that had few peers in the world. The other factor was that this late in the night — or very early morning — except for the occasional enormous truck-tractors, there was hardly any traffic.

Germain sped along keeping the Continental in sight, wishing it were daylight so the Continental would have to stay within the legal driving speeds. He made up his mind, if it looked as though the Continental were going to leave him altogether, he would signal the C.H.P. that the Continental was in violation of the speeding regulations. That way, Germain would not lose his man. Of course it wasn't really cricket, but then Germain was not playing a game.

It turned out not to be necessary. The closer they got to the city the more little outlying towns they had to pass through with large warning signs about speeding through. Each time the Continental slackened off, Germain was able to give Moore's car a deserved breathing spell. Finally, with the smell of the Bay Area reaching out unmistakably, and with those wayside towns closer together, the Continental dropped down considerably in speed. Germain was then able to keep pace without his stomach being in a knot. Also, he was getting steadily closer to the fringe-area for S.F.P.D. radio transmission.

He tested three times before he picked up a city radio receiving unit. He identified himself, asked that Sergeant Moore be notified that Inspector Germain was trailing a brown Continental towards the Bay Bridge, gave the licence number, and asked that Sergeant Moore confirm that an

155

interception was planned.

After that, with damp palms and a weary spirit, Germain slipped into the light, and for a change, welcome, traffic pattern which forced the Continental to slow still more, and from six cars back kept his prey in sight.

It was a lot later than Germain thought. If he'd looked at his wrist he'd have been surprised. He instead looked at his face in the rear-view mirror and saw the bluish beard-shadow as well as the sunken eyes, and that told him even more than a watch would have anyway. He had been actively involved and on his feet — or his seat — more than twenty-four hours. He smiled at the sinister face in the mirror.

'What a nice total of overtime — for which you don't get a thin dime.'

The face in the mirror winked, and Germain began the long-spending curve in the highway that would end up ahead a few miles, where the roadway straightened out, and where the wide entrance to the world-famous Golden Gate Bridge began. There, Moore should either be establishing his interception check-point in person, or he should have city cars doing that.

The radio crackled. A masculine voice said: 'Inspector Allan Germain, contact. Inspector Allan Germain, contact, please.'

He plucked the mouthpiece off its dashboard hook, watching the brown Continental up ahead making the curve. 'Germain here.' He said it twice and depressed the thumb-button. At once the pleasant masculine voice spoke again. 'Interception being established. Sergeant Moore on his way. Please identify yourself to officers at site. Clear?'

It was clear. Germain said so, hooked the rubber cup back on the dashboard and used both hands on the wheel as he began straightening out as the curve eased off.

The traffic in the four opposite lanes, which was northbound out of the city, was three or four times as heavy as incoming traffic, and the closer they got to the bridge, Moore's car and Scarpino's Continental, the more this became true.

157

Germain saw the awesome steel framework of the bridge up ahead, lighted, reddish coloured and toweringly high. He dropped his gaze to the brown Continental. Soon now it was going to be obvious to its driver that there was a police road-block up ahead, but the way the highway was made it would be almost impossible for the Continental to turn back. Not impossible, just *almost* impossible. That was what Germain assumed as his final obligation in the long high-speed race he was about to conclude; if the Continental's driver tried to swing around and race away, it would be up to Germain to ditch him.

It didn't happen. The Continental's driver either saw the road-block too late, or he had no reason to fear it. As the cars ahead of him slowed to a crawl and were passed on through by several black-uniformed officers, the Continental kept its place in line and went closer as though it had no reason to fear an interception.

Germain allowed himself the luxury of a big yawn just before the Continental pulled up, halted, and a police officer approached it from both sides. Germain eased out of the traffic to the right side of the bridge approach, climbed stiffly from Sergeant Moore's car, stretched, then walked on over where the uniformed man was talking to the greying, rather bulky man in the Continental.

A swarthy uniformed sergeant stepped up in front of Germain to block his progress. He looked perfectly capable of handling just about any kind of trouble that came his way. Germain fished forth his identification folder, held it to the light, and said his name. The sergeant smiled. 'Did you shag that Lincoln all the way down the inland highway?'

Germain nodded while pocketing his I.D. folder. 'And it turned my hair white doing it,' he said.

They went over where the uniformed men were standing back to allow the greying, angry driver of the Continental room to climb out. More officers moved in. One slid into the Continental to move it out of the line of traffic. The other officer waved the cars that were waiting on through.

As the sergeant and Inspector Germain walked over, the sergeant made a motion to the protesting prisoner. 'Turn,' he ordered. 'Lean on the car top, push your feet back — and shut up!'

Germain waited while the bulky, greying man was frisked, and disarmed. He was carrying a .350 magnum revolver in a shoulder-holster. It had a two-and-a-half inch reinforced barrel. There was no more deadly revolver in the world.

Germain loosened his tie and rubbed a scratchy jaw. He guessed the greying man's name from the café proprietress's general description and comments. As soon as the frisking was completed he said, 'Good morning, Mario. You'd make a good race driver.'

The shorter, thicker man dropped his arms, stared hard at Germain, then shook his head. 'Mister, I don't know you. But if you're a cop and you're mixed up in this roust, take my word for it, you're in all kinds of trouble.'

Germain said, 'Sure. I'm always in trouble when I lend a hand in apprehending people carrying that kind of artillery. I suppose you have a concealed-weapons permit?'

Mario sneered. 'Oh, for Christ's sake grow up, will you? Nobody gets pinched for that any more. If that's it, then I'll post a cash bond and be on my way.'

The uniformed sergeant and Mario exchanged a stare. The uniformed officer was a different kind of cop and Mario either knew it from experience or sensed it, because when the sergeant pointed towards a police car with a wired-in rear compartment, Mario didn't even act like he might protest.

The uniformed officer handed Germain the .350 magnum. 'Sergeant Moore said he'd be waiting in his office. They'll take him there. You can ride with them if you'd like, Inspector.'

Germain would have liked that, but he had to return Moore's car. He thanked the uniformed officer and went back to the parked vehicle, climbed in and punched the starter. If he never had to drive Sergeant Moore's car one more mile it would please him immensely.

13

Mario In The Sweatbox!

Sergeant Moore was waiting. As soon as the prisoner and Inspector Germain arrived he got them both a cup of coffee from the night-duty wardroom. He had a teletype message on his desk which he glanced at as he said, 'Mario, you know the law about ex-convicts owning or carrying firearms.'

The bulky, greying man shook his head almost affably. He was sitting, sipping black coffee as though this were a conventional meeting among friends or associates.

'Okay. I broke a law. It's a misdemeanour.'

Sergeant Moore eased down upon the edge of his desk. 'No; it'll be rougher than a misdemeanour, Mario. It'll be aiding and abetting a fugitive in flight to avoid prosecution.'

Mario studied Moore, then turned and frowned at Germain. 'What's he talking about — aiding and abetting a fugitive? What fugitive? You guys know where I've spent the whole damned summer? You wouldn't believe this, but — '

'Murder,' said Allan Germain, softly, but Mario heard, and his voice went dead in mid-sentence while he sat staring.

'Murder!' Mario glanced at Germain. 'What murder?'

'A man named Foster Hellner back in Chicago,' replied Germain. 'Joe Buono hit him at the Chicago airport.'

To Germain, and evidently to Sergeant Moore also, Mario's astonishment was genuine. When the moment of total shock passed, Mario lifted the cup, drained it, then leaned to put it on the desk, leaned back to light a cigarette, and continued his long study of Germain. Finally he said, 'Who are you, Mister?'

Germain brought forth his I.D. folder and held it up. 'Inspector Germain, Chicago P.D.'

Mario sighed and looked up at Moore. 'On the level?' he asked, but he knew the answer without Moore answering. 'Who the hell's Foster Hellner? I never heard of him. Why would Joe Buono want to hit him?'

Germain answered. 'Hellner tried to bomb the flight out of Chicago, to Denver, Joe Buono was taking. We don't know how Buono discovered Hellner's connection to the bomb, but that's only a detail. We know what happened after Buono discovered that connection; he killed Hellner.'

Moore kept studying the prisoner. 'Where is Buono?' he asked. 'Look, Mario, we have a pretty fair idea what he's doing here. If you protect him you're equally guilty in the eyes of the law.'

Mario sneered. 'Guilty of what; visiting San Francisco?' But Mario's attitude had changed. 'Look, I know my rights. I want a lawyer to be present during this interrogation. I want to post bond.'

Sergeant Moore looked at Germain a bit sardonically as he answered. 'Okay, there's a telephone. You're entitled to make one call. Too bad you can't reach Scarpino's mountaintop.' Moore stood up off the side of the desk and yawned, and as Mario left his chair to go to the telephone Moore, acting indifferent, jerked his head at Germain and went back by the rear-wall window. 'Hit him like a ton of bricks,' he confided to Germain in a low murmur. You know what I think, Inspector? I think Joe Buono hit your man Hellner without any authorization at all, and I don't think he told anyone he did it.'

Germain had arrived at the same conclusions after viewing Mario's astonishment. 'I wish that had been Angelo Scarpino sitting there; I'd like to see his face when he learns that the assassin he imported so carefully had the law trailing him halfway across the country because of a senseless killing.'

Moore stood gazing over where Mario Spina was talking to someone on the telephone and ignoring the conferring detectives as though they did not exist. 'I'll put a surveillance team on him as soon as his lawyer shows up to post bond.'

To Germain this was routine, but he

did not believe Mario would lead them to Joe Buono. Not now; Mario would know he was under surveillance. Men like Mario knew all the tricks and all the rules. 'He's going out to the airport, Sergeant, to hire someone to fly him back to the mountaintop. We just put a bee in his ear.'

Sergeant Moore's clinical interest made him say, 'One way or another, from here on out, he's going to be working for us, like it or not, and he'll know that. But what I want from him is Buono's address here in the city.'

Mario put aside the telephone, lit a fresh cigarette and glanced up where Germain and Moore were standing. 'Lawyer'll be here in a little while,' he said, blowing smoke. He looked longest at Inspector Germain. 'Why would anybody shoot a guy for trying to plant a bomb on an aeroplane?'

Germain had only his own personal approximation about that, but he gave it as though it were pure fact. 'Because the bomber had already planted his bomb, and because it was on Buono's flight, and no one likes being blown up in mid-air.'

'How did he know the lousy bomb had been planted?'

Germain had to reach a little for an answer, but he made the effort because he wanted Mario to take all this back to Scarpino. The *reason* he wanted it taken back was not just spite, but it *was* unprofessional: He wanted Scarpino to react against Buono, which he thought would happen if Scarpino understood how Buono's senseless killing had jeopardized Scarpino. Obviously, Buono had omitted mention of the Chicago killing. His reason for doing that was not difficult to understand; he was supposed to be coming to the West Coast to do a job for Scarpino, and he was *not* supposed to do anything along the way that would cause attention to be directed towards himself *or* Scarpino.

Mario scowled. 'I asked you a question, Inspector. How did he know the bomb was on his flight?'

'He saw the nut plant it.'

Mario leaned to stub out his half-smoked cigarette. 'He didn't have to kill no one. He could have just taken a later flight.'

Germain shook his head. 'You know better, Mario. He was on a tight schedule. If he fouled up in Chicago the itinerary would be fouled up all down the line. He wouldn't have arrived on Scarpino's mountain on time, would he?'

Mario leaned back and studied Germain from troubled eyes. 'Chicago detective, eh,' he mused.

Germain knew what came next. Evidently Sergeant Moore did also because he strolled to the desk to retrieve his coffee cup without looking at either man again until after Germain shook his head at Mario. 'There will be no compromise, Mario. You can have someone go over my head to the bureau chief in Chicago, but it'll be a dry run, I can tell you that in advance.'

Mario looked at his watch and fell silent. He was not, obviously, a person who made decisions. He was a Mafia soldier, a leg-man, messenger, bodyguard, even upon occasion an assassin within the organization, but his limitations were known and he was not authorized to exceed them. He would not exceed them either; the rules were strict and Mario was the type of person who, having enforced them himself, would never move unless told to do so by his superiors, in this case Angelo Scarpino.

Moore looked into Mario's empty cup and said, 'More coffee?'

Mario flicked him a look and shook his head. He was deep in private thought.

Moore eased down behind the desk. 'Mario, we want to know where Joe Buono is.'

Mario's expression was cold and contemptuous. 'Sure you do. Fat lot of good wanting to know will do you.'

Moore's expression did not change but the sound of his voice did. 'Don't get too wise,' he told Spina. 'Your lawyer can tell you that if we think it's advisable we can request that you be held without bail in the public interest.'

Mario sat a moment looking from Moore to Germain, then back again. His attitude changed a little. 'I don't know where he is.'

'But he's here in the city,' said Moore, 'and his target is Hale Buchanan, the City Attorney.' It wasn't a question, at least it wasn't said that way although the pause afterwards left plenty of latitude for that kind of interpretation.

'There's nothing I can tell you,' replied Mario, and looked impatiently at his watch. 'What's keeping that lousy lawyer?'

Moore said, 'It's not daylight yet. You probably got him out of bed.'

Mario was unconcerned. 'They're on retainers and they get plenty.'

Moore looked up as Germain went to a chair and sat down. Mario also gazed at the Chicago detective, but his stare was baleful, as though all this was Inspector Germain's fault.

Germain said, in a pleasant tone of voice, he thought he would ask that Mario be held without bail. For a moment there wasn't a sound in the office. Mario fished out his limp packet of smokes and lit another one. Except for this chain-smoking he did not appear particularly nervous. He was angry, that was very clear, and he was also upset although he managed to minimise the outward evidence of it. To Germain, Mario seemed to be a man with his back to a wall; this was what Germain was working on.

'If Buono hits the City Attorney,' he said pleasantly to Spina, 'we can take your boss into court and prove that Buono visited the mountaintop; that the very next day he was brought down here, by air, Mario, and that he came with obvious instructions to kill Buchanan.'

'Obvious isn't good enough,' growled Spina. 'You got to have proof. I know that much law.'

Germain smiled. 'Okay, we'll get that too. But let's say we don't get it. Buono is still wanted in Chicago on a murder warrant. Your boss gave sanctuary to a wanted fugitive. How will the Council like it — having Angelo Scarpino himself brought into court on a charge that implies he is a foolish old man, so foolish he could be made to look like he's slipping? Mario, how will *Scarpino* like that?'

Germain had touched a raw spot; this,

apparently, was exactly what Mario had been sitting there fuming about. And it wasn't all family loyalty either, although with a man like Mario Spina that had to be a large part of it; the rest of it was more basic: If Angelo Scarpino, Mario's chieftain, were rebuked or had some, even perhaps most, of his power and authority taken away, Mario's standing would also suffer.

But Mario's first enemy was the police. The organization took care of its own, one way or another. Whether Mario liked what he saw coming or not, he could not, either in conscience or otherwise, do anything at all that would help his foremost enemy, so he sat and glared at Germain, trapped and troubled by an event that was becoming to appear more and more pointless, the killing of a psychopath in Chicago.

Germain, satisfied now that Joe Buono had not told Angelo Scarpino of the Chicago murder because, by the time he arrived on the West Coast he realized it had been a mistake, saw that Hellner killing as his best opportunity to exploit a crack in the Cosa Nostra's armour. With that in mind he kept working on Mario.

'Give us Joe Buono,' he said. 'Mario, use your head. We're going to get him anyway, but we'd rather do it before he makes matters worse for all of us. Tell us where to find him and go on back to Scarpino so you'll be hundreds of miles away and can't be tied to whatever happens down here.'

Mario was adamant, but troubled. 'I can't do that. It's not up to me.'

Moore made a suggestion. 'If this lawyer posts bond and you walk out of here, Mario, and our City Attorney gets killed by the man you and Scarpino aided in his flight to avoid prosecution, I can promise you even the Attorney General's office will be down on you so hard the best criminal lawyer in the world won't be able to get you off the hook.'

Mario smoked his cigarette to the filter and put it out. 'Where is that damned lawyer?' he snarled.

Moore gestured. 'Call Scarpino. Inspector Germain and I'll leave you alone in here. Scarpino will tell you to give Buono to us.'

Mario exploded. 'Call hell! There's no telephone on that stupid mountain. The only way we knew anything was when that lunkhead with the chopper flew in. And you guys have queered that too, haven't you?'

Sergeant Moore nodded. He and Germain waited for Mario's turmoil to lessen. It didn't, but Mario finally made a decision, a very painful one because he was not a person to whom decision-making came easily.

He looked squarely at Allan Germain and said, 'Look, don't louse up the bond and I'll go back and talk to Mr Scarpino. That's all I can do.'

Germain had an answer ready. 'Okay . . . And I go back with you.'

Even Sergeant Moore was startled. He and Mario stared, and Germain raised his head as the sound of footfalls beyond the door sounded loudly in the hush. Someone knocked, Sergeant Moore called for them to enter, and one look at the dapper, greying man who came into the office was enough to let all three seated men know that the lawyer had finally arrived.

Mario barely looked up as the lawyer introduced himself. Mario leaned and said, 'Okay, Chicago, you come back with me.'

14

Face-To-Face On The Mountaintop

Sergeant Moore had mixed feelings. While Mario and his lawyer was conferring, Moore took Germain to the back window and said, 'What's the point? Spina will tell Scarpino the whole story.'

Germain did not dispute that. 'Maybe, but he sure as hell won't tell it the way you or I would. I'll be safe enough.'

Moore agreed on principle. 'I doubt that he'd have you leaned on now if you hit him, but the point is, we're no closer to Buono than before.'

Germain frowned. 'You're wrong. We're just one helicopter ride forth and back from Buono. If Scarpino is only half as smart as I think he is, he'll hand us Buono on a silver platter.'

Moore, whose protest had been weak at best, said, 'Okay. I'll check out a transceiver for you to take along.'

Germain said there was no need, that if he had to get in contact with San Francisco he would do it through the helicopter transmitter, and Sergeant Moore smiled.

'It's too early in the morning for me to be functioning. Fair enough. I'll have one of our men out there to monitor calls. By the way — good luck, Inspector.'

Germain nodded. 'Just keep the drag-net dragging. You'll probably come up with our boy before I get back. Incidentally, what's the latest on the City Attorney?'

'He's coming back tonight, on a late flight. Berryman will be with him.' Moore turned as the lawyer said his name. Mario was standing, and he was puffing on another cigarette, his fourth or fifth since entering the office. The lawyer wanted to know what charges would be filed. Moore shrugged, 'It's a fluid situation. A lot of it depends upon Mario and his boss. For the time being I'll put in for a warrant but hold it in abeyance.'

'What kind of warrant?'

'Aiding and abetting.'

The lawyer flicked a glance past at Allan Germain. 'Proof?' he said.

Sergeant Moore showed his first irascibility of the new day when he said, 'Look, the disclosure law doesn't extend to my damned office. If you want to file for bail-bond that's your business, but you'd better read it off the registry downstairs when I book your client, and until then butt out.'

The lawyer was not the least perturbed. He turned towards Mario. 'You don't have to come back, and you'll be out of his jurisdiction up there. He'll have to go through the sheriff of that county where the summer place is and extradite you just as though — '

'Save it,' growled Mario. 'Hey, Chicago, you ready to go?'

Germain was ready. The four of them left Moore's office. Somewhere on the mezzanine floor the lawyer disappeared without being missed, but Sergeant Moore took them out to the airport in his departmental car and remained with them until Germain had engaged a charter chopper, smaller and older than the elegant Alouette, and also a more subdued colour. At the door Sergeant Moore shook his head at Germain, then grinned. 'Crazy,' he called, and ran back as the sweep-blades began rotating. Mario looked as though he might have agreed, but their pilot, a slit-lipped, squint-eyed, piratical-looking older man, the only outsider who had heard Moore say that, wasn't interested at all. He acted as though he were a heart-surgeon studying all the mechanical aids to his profession when the rotors were winding up. Then, without more than a sidelong glance to be certain his passengers were harnessed in, he lifted his craft, swung it, and went beating his way north-eastwards into the cool dawn.

Mario was a glum companion and the pilot was an indifferent one; his entire concentration was riveted upon what he was doing, which was indisputably for the best; even a helicopter would not be able to land safely in most of the country they had to fly over.

Germain would have enjoyed the low-level flight more if he hadn't had so many other things on his mind. He did not worry much about the City Attorney being assassinated; he felt that Sergeant Moore had that well in hand. What *did* trouble him was Joe Buono. All he knew for a fact was that Buono was an uninhibited killer. If Buono got wind of the fact that the police were seriously seeking him, he would not be the least bit reluctant about killing anyone who got between him and escape, including any luckless private citizens.

There was another angle too. If Buono found out that Angelo Scarpino knew about the Chicago murder, before the police could apprehend and disarm Joe Buono, it was anyone's guess how he would react.

In summary, Joe Buono the professional killer, was the crux. Even if Scarpino handed him over to the police, he would still have to be apprehended. Sergeant Moore was experienced, Germain did not question that at all, but the initiative would in all probability not lie with Moore, it would lie with the murderer, and if there was one type of person on earth who was reliably unpredictable it was a man without a conscience, but who otherwise was probably as intelligent as any other person.

The helicopter banked and their grim-lipped pilot pointed downward and ahead. 'That it?' he asked.

Mario grunted. 'Yeah. Circle twice before you let down. You got that?'

The pilot nodded and banked to make twin sweeps, low and wide. Germain thought he saw someone standing just within the foremost fringe of trees across the meadow in the direction of the A-frame chalet, but when they made their second banking turn he was less sure.

Their pilot came down smoothly, hovered six feet, then eased down all the way. He did not cut his motor but after both passengers had alighted he leaned towards Germain and said, 'Want me to wait or come back?' His hand hovered near a toggle-switch.

Germain said, 'Wait,' and the hand fell, throwing the switch that interrupted the ignition. At once the chopper's great blades whined down as they unwound.

Mario was out where the wind from the blades was worst. He waited impatiently for Germain, and looked in the other direction only when a man in laced-boots and suntan trousers came across the meadow. By the time Germain got over beside Mario the other man was close enough to look swiftly from Mario to Germain, in a most uncompromising manner.

Mario said, 'Benny, stay with the chopper-guy. Keep him in that thing. I've got to take this guy to see Mr Scarpino.'

Benny was medium size, but thin. He looked more boy than man despite the furrowed brow and lined mouth. His dark eyes were expressionless even when they rested upon Mario. 'What happened?' he asked. 'Where's the car?'

Mario's temper was very near the surface, and had been for some time now. 'The car is all right,' he said. 'The rest, I'll tell you about later. Now stay with the damned chopper.'

Germain trudged across the meadow behind Mario. He had already admired the lake from the air, and now he admired it again from the ground. He also liked the crisp coolness of this high, isolated place, the fragrance of the forest when he followed Mario across it to the clearing where he had a closer look at the structure he'd previously looked upon from far overhead, and the overhead blue sky.

The thick, round, massive man leaning upon the porch railing as Mario and Germain emerged from forest-shade, was wearing leather sandals, a platinum wristwatch, tinted sunglasses, and a net shirt with short sleeves that hung outside his trousers. Germain recognized the coarse features but he was shocked at how much heavier Angelo Scarpino was face-to-face than he looked in his photographs. It dawned on Germain only as Mario glumly led the way up the outdoor stairs to the porch above, that the reason he had not expected such a grossly overweight person was because he had never seen a photograph of Scarpino that showed more than head and shoulders. Now he understood why.

Also, Scarpino was shorter than Germain had expected him to be. When he turned to stare impassively at Germain, he had to tilt his head.

Mario sounded sulky when he said, 'Mr Scarpino, this is a detective from Chicago. His name is Germain.'

Scarpino looked steadily at Mario without acknowledging the introduction for a long moment. Mario made a fluttery gesture. 'I didn't know what else to do, Mr Scarpino.'

'You didn't know what else to do about *what*?' Scarpino demanded in a flat voice.

Germain took it up. 'Your man, Joe Buono, shot and killed a man in Chicago on his way out here, Mr Scarpino. I picked up his trail there and it led me here.'

Scarpino stared. 'What are you talking about?'

Germain did not repeat it. 'Chicago has a warrant outstanding. The San Francisco Police Department will co-operate in the extradition proceedings. But — we want Buono before he hits Hale Buchanan.'

Angelo Scarpino blinked, continued to stand there studying Allan Germain for a bit longer, then he turned and said, 'Come inside, Mr Germain. Mario, you come inside too.'

Germain did not appreciate the taste-fulness of the interior furnishings; he was concentrating on his host. He had handed Scarpino a low blow, he was sure of that. He was also certain that once they sat down, Scarpino would reveal whichever attitude he would take henceforth.

It was cooler inside. There was a large spray of wildflowers on a window-ledge where sunshine came through like liquid gold. Scarpino turned, pointed to the chair nearest Germain, and sat opposite him. Mario sat farther back and to one side, he was being his customary diffident self. He still looked decidedly unhappy.

'Now,' said Angelo Scarpino, 'start at the beginning, Mr Germain. How do you know Joe Buono killed a man in Chicago; how do you even know it was Joe Buono?'

Germain could answer those two questions rather easily and convincingly. There were other questions he would have to be vague about, but not those two. When he'd finished speaking he could see the colour rising in Angelo Scarpino's layered neck. Germain threw his next verbal punch.

'Buono doesn't have to tell us you sent for him, Mr Scarpino. He can even deny it if he'd care to. The basis for a warrant against you will be aiding and abetting a fugitive seeking to avoid prosecution for suspicion of murder.'

Scarpino stared at Germain, removed his sunglasses and set them aside. 'Who was this man Joe supposedly shot?'

'Foster Hellner.'

'Who's he?'

Germain didn't answer the question. 'That's not important. Buono killed him and we can prove it. *That's* important. Then Buono flew directly here to see you. We can also prove that. Finally, the same helicopter took him back down to San Francisco, Mr Scarpino. We have a pretty reliable idea about what he's doing down there, and who he is supposed to hit.'

Angelo Scarpino was recovering from the surprise of all this; he was not as liable to shock as Mario had been. In fact, he even smiled at Germain.

'Look; Mr Germain, I practically raised Joe Buono. He comes to see me down in Florida maybe two, three times a year. He could do the same up here. I'm not saying he *did*, I'm only saying he could. He's been like a son to me.'

Germain smiled right back. 'Some son to do a trick like that to you. Mr Scarpino, if he's successful down in San Francisco, if he makes even a small ripple down there, your neck will be in the noose right along with his. But maybe what's even worse, if he kills the City Attorney, you are implicated as an accessory.'

Scarpino flung thick arms wide. 'Me? Look, Mr Germain, I don't even know the City Attorney out here.' Scarpino levered himself up to his full height and smiled again. 'A glass of wine before you leave?'

Germain also rose. So did Mario, who had not said a word since they'd entered the house; who had watched first his chief, then the detective from Chicago.

Germain made his offer. 'Give us Buono, Mr Scarpino, before he makes an attempt on the City Attorney, and he goes back to Chicago for that stupid murder and you are out of it.' Germain stood returning Scarpino's stare. The older, much fatter man slowly shook his head.

'I don't know where Joe Buono is,' he told Germain. 'Okay, you don't have to believe me, but that happens to be the truth.'

Germain did not believe it. 'Where was Mario going in your Continental, Mr Scarpino?'

The Mafia chieftain's eyes showed fire. 'I don't answer questions for the police. I got lawyers for that, Germain. Mario's got a right to go anywhere. As for my cars, I loan them to anyone, all the time. Look, you don't have anything, Mr Chicago Detective.' That ended it as far as Scarpino was concerned. He turned and beckoned to Mario, and as the bulky man moved forward Scarpino said, 'Go out on the porch, Mr Germain. Admire the view.'

Germain did just exactly that, but primarily because he wanted a breath of fresh air. He thought he had seen that look on a man's face, in there, that he had seen before. He thought he also knew why Angelo Scarpino had refused to trade Joe Buono for his own safety. Right then, as Germain halted at the porch railing to gaze off down through the trees towards the meadow and the blue-water lake, Angelo Scarpino was giving an order to Mario Spina; it concerned the man down in San Francisco Scarpino had said was like a son to him. Germain could almost imagine the words themselves.

'Find him, Mario, and hit him! Look what he did to me. Shot some nothing in Chicago and didn't mention it. Now look what he's got me in. Take care of that, Mario!'

15

It's A Big City

Germain had failed and he was conscious of it. As he and Mario went trudging back down through the trees to the helicopter he said, 'Well, it was a good try, Mario.'

The greying, lumpy man didn't even look around. He walked along as though his thoughts were a million miles away.

Germain let it stay like that until they came forth upon the emerald meadow and could see the chopper, Benny keeping his impassive vigil, and beyond, that exquisite blue-water lake. Then Germain spoke once again.

'I thought he had more sense than to let a punk like Buono set him up, Mario. That's what's happening; you know that don't you?'

Mario kept on walking as he gruffly said, 'All I know is that I've got to bring his car back. That's *all*, so why don't you quit bugging me, Inspector?'

Germain took no heed of the warning. 'Joe Buono was like a son to him. How many fathers get used like that? Did you see his face, Mario, when I told him Buono had killed a man on his way out here, and hadn't told him about it?'

Mario stopped and whirled, angry all over. 'I said get off my back!'

Germain came around loose and slouched. 'If you'd get smart I'd be glad to. Mario, you're going down the drain with Buono and Scarpino. Did you know that?'

Mario's face was strained and splotchy. 'Get in that damned chopper,' he snarled, 'and shut up, or I'll break your lousy jaw. Now go on, get in there!'

Germain smiled very deliberately. 'Try it, Mario. Try breaking my jaw.'

The charter-pilot and Benny saw them arguing out on the meadow. Germain was aware of this, but it seemed that Mario was even more conscious of it, because, fury or no fury, he turned and rushed the remaining distance. There, he jerked his head at Benny. 'Go on back now. I'll see you as soon as I can drive Mr Scarpino's car back.'

Benny moved out without looking back. Mario stepped up into the chopper and Germain stepped up right behind him. The pilot waited until the door was secured and until the flight-harnesses were buckled, then he ground some life into his rotors. He didn't say a word and he didn't act at all perturbed about having been under guard while he waited. If Germain had looked the man over more closely, he might have read something from the lipless mouth and the sunk-set, tough eyes. Their charter-pilot had been a Marine Corps aviator.

The lift off was smooth. They made one big circle of the meadow and as they beat their way southward over the top of Angelo Scarpino's A-frame residence, Germain could look almost straight down and see Scarpino standing on the porch, glass in hand and sunglasses back in place, watching their over-flight.

There was an increasing heat haze the farther down-country they flew. It was very pleasant at their altitude but obviously it was a very hot day in the city, bay or no bay.

Germain was hungry. He hadn't thought about being tired or in need of a shave, for hours. He didn't think of those things now, either, but hunger was something a person could never very successfully ignore.

Mario surprised him by leaning and yelling in his ear. 'You blew it, didn't you?'

Germain could afford to be magnanimous and allow Mario this skimpy bit of consolation. 'Sure did. But *he* blew it worse. As soon as we nail Buono I'll fly back in there with a warrant and bring him out for booking and jail.'

Mario shook his head, almost smiling. 'You'll never lay a hand on Angelo Scarpino. Never. I don't give a damn how many warrants you get or how many witnesses you bring up.'

Germain had not wished to dispute such an extravagant claim, especially when to do so he would have to yell above the noise of their conveyance. He turned back to studying the terrain down below.

The mountains did not do as most mountains did, rise up gradually after being preceded by increasingly high hills. They instead stood back near the northern end of a tapering valley, and quite suddenly reared up blue-tinted with forest cover, and behind the helicopter, and slightly northward, was that huge mountain with the snow streamers down its bony and stony flanks. Beyond, there seemed to be more mountains until the horizon curved and Germain could see no further. It was an experience, and a view, he would never forget, flying over this unknown one-third of California.

The helicopter-pilot used his radio when San Francisco was still no more than a smoke-blot of gigantic size on the distant, shimmering horizon. He called for clearance to the control tower, identified himself, and a moment later he leaned to poke his microphone over at Germain. Sergeant Moore himself was on the other end. He said, 'Any luck?'

Germain answered in one word. 'None. Have you had any?'

Moore answered even more brusquely.

'No. I'll be waiting with a car at the pad.'

That was all that was said until they beat down to an elevation no fixed-wing aircraft would have dared at low speed, and Germain saw the private landing area that was their destination.

Their pilot did exactly as he had done at the mountaintop; he flew directly over his parking site then dropped to within six feet of the ground, hovered a moment, then eased down so gently that if the tail section hadn't rocked back his passengers wouldn't have known they were on the ground. No doubt about it, the charter-pilot was very experienced, and right then Germain couldn't have cared less.

He stepped down, saw Sergeant Moore standing off a respectable distance, out of the way of the rotor propwash, turned to wait for Mario to also alight, then he and Mario went over to where Moore stood.

For a moment it was a little awkward. No matter how the three of them conferred, or even sat shoulder-to-shoulder in a helicopter or a police car, they were dedicated and unflinching enemies. Mario said, 'I'm to have that lawyer post bond. Then I'm to drive Mr Scarpino's car back.'

Mario stared at Sergeant Moore as though positive there would be some kind of duel, but Moore simply shrugged Mario off and raised an eyebrow at Germain. The answer to that look was only slightly more elaborate than Germain had given over the radio.

'It was a good idea, Sergeant, it just didn't work. Scarpino won't trade Buono for non-involvement.'

Mario started to say something about that but Moore turned. 'Head for the car,' he said. 'Talk later.'

Mario obeyed, walking grumpily along. Behind him Germain and Sergeant Moore exchanged a look and Germain gravely inclined his head.

None of them spoke on the drive back to police headquarters but the moment they had left the car and approached the massive doors of the stone building, Mario said, 'I'll make the call from the booking desk.'

Moore did not discourage that. Whether he would have been entitled to or not was moot; under the law he had technically complied with arrest-procedure by permitting Mario one telephone call after apprehension. Also, Mario had not been booked, so actually he was not under legal restraint.

But these were issues few policemen heeded; lawyers might, but Sergeant Moore and Inspector Germain were thinking along a different line. They went aside as Mario asked to use one of the booking officer's telephones, and Moore said, 'Anything?'

Germain smiled crookedly. 'I've been playing hunches for a week now. I'll play one more; Scarpino spoke privately to Spina just before we left. My hunch is that he passed Mario the contract on Joe Buono.'

'Did Scarpino act like he knew where Buono is?'

Germain shook his head. 'He played it so straight I almost believed him. He wouldn't buy any part of my suggestion. That leaves him in a bad spot and he knows it — but — if he has Buono iced, then we have no case at all, have we? Even the Chicago warrant is worthless against a dead man.'

Sergeant Moore gazed over where Mario was frowning and speaking into the telephone. 'Okay, I've got a surveillance team ready to take over the minute Mario walks out of here. But while I was standing around out at the airport waiting, I got to wondering if I would do this, were I in Scarpino's shoes. Mario isn't that qualified as a hit-man.'

Germain gave a coldly practical reply to that. 'Scarpino doesn't give a damn, right now. He's moving scairt and if he loses both his boys, just as long as we have no case, it's worth it in his eyes.'

Moore rolled that around, then said, 'Nice guy, Angelo Scarpino.'

Germain shrugged. 'Of all the things he's been accused of I don't think that's ever been one of them.'

Mario finished his telephone call just as Germain asked Moore how the search was coming and got a sour look. 'Don't even ask,' grumbled Moore, and eyed Mario as he replaced the telephone. Moore then led the way up to his office.

Mario would have lit a cigarette but his pack was empty. He crumpled it, hurled it into a basket beside the desk and accepted the pack Germain dropped upon the desk without even nodding. As he lit up he said, 'The lawyer'll be around in a short while.' He exhaled smoke. 'And of course you guys'll have a tail on me from the minute I walk out the front door.'

Moore smiled a bit thinly. 'That's how the game is played, isn't it, Mario?'

Germain didn't give Mario much chance to answer, but it was improbable that he would have, anyway. Germain went to lean upon the wall and gaze dispassionately at the bulky, greying man.

'You're not up to it, Mario,' he said. 'You wouldn't stand a prayer of a chance and I think you know it.'

Mario squinted at Moore. 'What's he talking about?'

Moore picked up the telephone and punched one of the little lighted buttons as though he hadn't been addressed. Germain spoke, blurring the sound of

Moore's voice and spoiling Mario's chances of eavesdropping.

'Mario, I'll give you my opinion. Scarpino set you up. Not deliberately, but it amounts to the same thing because he knows as well as you and I do that you're not in Joe Buono's league.'

Mario squinted again. 'You're not making a lick of sense. You know that don't you? What league? How does a man set someone up and not do it deliberately?'

'When he told you to come back down here and hit Buono,' answered Germain.

Mario rolled up his eyes in a simulation of monumental exasperation. 'Man, you're talking right off the top of your skull. Joe Buono is like Mr Scarpino's son.'

'If you find him,' said Germain, boring right in despite Spina's disgust, 'the only way you'll get to him, Mario, is by being his old buddy and walking right up when he's not expecting anything. Otherwise, if he is suspicious at all, you're a dead duck.'

200

Moore put down the telephone, listened to Germain and Spina for a moment while watching the shorter and bulkier man, then he leaned upon the desk and shot Germain a glance. 'They may have picked up something out near the airport,' he said, sounding casual. Then he shrugged. 'But it's a big city and one man can look pretty much like another one.'

Ten minutes later the lawyer arrived. He had posted bond and Mario was free to go. They left together, Moore alerted someone downstairs, and Germain went out in search of some black coffee. When he returned Sergeant Moore was on the telephone. The tempo of the search was beginning to pick up.

The desk clerk at a mid-town hotel made a positive identification of Joe Buono from a police photograph, but that only proved where Buono had been because he had left the hotel, had checked out, right after breakfast, and the desk clerk had no idea where he had gone.

Germain asked about the airport and

Sergeant Moore sighed. 'Just spreading a little confusion around, when I said that, so the survillance team can get accustomed to Mario's behaviour-pattern.' Moore considered Germain a moment then said, 'Why don't you go to your hotel and get some sleep? At least shave. You look more like a Mafia assassin than Joe Buono does.'

Germain laughed, felt his face, decided Moore was right, and finished his coffee before departing. Moore promised to telephone him at the hotel if anything very promising turned up.

Until Germain was out of the building in the sunglare, searching his mind for an answer to what Scarpino would do if Mario failed to find Buono, he didn't become aware that the morning was gone and afternoon had arrived. He glanced at his watch, listened to make certain it hadn't stopped, then put everything out of his mind as he hiked for his hotel, and up there, with the noise of the city rather muted by height, he used the shower first, then he shaved because he did not expect to actually sleep very long, and finally he went to bed at an hour that would ordinarily have seemed incongruous to say the least, and barely got his eyes closed before sleep arrived.

16

The Walking Bomb

It has been said that sleep is cumulative; that a man can postpone it for a long while, and when he finally does go to bed he will sleep for hours on end until his system is re-generated.

That may be true, but Allan Germain had no chance to put it to a test because when the telephone on his night-stand rang a little over four hours after he had returned, and although he had a bit of a struggle coming awake, shaking out the cobwebs, the moment he heard Sergeant Moore's voice he was wide awake.

'Mario evidently was telling the truth when he said he didn't know where Joe Buono was; he's been down at the airport except for a couple of local stops since he left my office. One of the stops was at a restaurant, the other one was when he called at a garage and had the plugs changed in Scarpino's Continental.'

Germain was not surprised that the Continental needed new ignition plugs. 'He drove that thing hard when I was tailing him down out of the mountains.'

Moore laughed. 'Maybe. But that garage happens to be the place where one of the local Cosa Nostra families has a contact. The surveillance team thinks Mario picked up a gun down there. They didn't see the transaction, but they saw him go into the office with the man who runs the garage, who is one of the family.'

Germain digested that. 'Then he probably passed the word about Joe Buono, and that could complicate things.'

Sergeant Moore wasn't too perturbed. 'Possibly, of course, except that the people I talked to in our intelligence unit are of the opinion that no local Cosa Nostra people will like the idea well enough to help. Unless, of course, they are ordered to do so. Intelligence is of the opinion that the local chieftains won't like the idea of Scarpino making ripples on the West Coast; they also think the locals will view this mess as Scarpino's private vendetta.'

Germain hoped the intelligence people were correct. He looked at his watch. It was almost six o'clock and he was hungry again. 'When does the City Attorney's plane arrive?'

'Midnight. You can go back to sleep if you'd like. I simply wanted you to know that Mario is armed again . . . If he gets too frustrated or impatient, he might decide to substitute one corpse for another — you, for example.'

Germain yawned, scratched his head and said, 'Nice thought. Okay; I'll get dressed and come on down.'

As he put down the telephone and climbed out of bed, Germain turned over this fresh possibility of assassination. It hardly seemed worth worrying about. Not that Spina would hesitate to shoot a detective, but if he allowed himself to be side-tracked by some personal animosity, he might miss finding Joe Buono. That would not sit at all well with Angelo Scarpino.

Germain showered, dressed, ran a hand

over his jaw to be reassured the earlier shave had been adequate, then he went downstairs to the dining-room, and for once had good enough timing to get fed. Afterwards, he walked out into the pleasant evening, caught the salt-scent of the bay, and liked the little breeze that was blowing steadily inland.

He was beginning to believe that Moore's valiant effort to find one needle in the huge haystack that was San Francisco, was not going to succeed. That left only one alternative; the airport.

Unless Joe Buono got scairt off, perhaps through the Cosa Nostra grapevine, if he knew any of the local members and they would pass along the warning about Mario and the police to him, he would know by now approximately who to expect at the airport, aside from the City Attorney.

For Sergeant Moore to seal off the airport building would be no hardship. It might be more difficult for plain clothes men to identify Buono among the hundreds of people circulating through the terminal building, but if he were on hand an hour or two before the City Attorney's flight touched down, they should be able to do that.

What would help greatly was the probability that Joe Buono, who had left Scarpino's mountaintop chalet before anyone but the police knew he was being sought, would not be exercising any more than the normal caution.

The possibility also existed, however, that Mario might have carried a message to the local chieftains, through that contact at the garage, and that whether Moore and the S.F.P.D. intelligence unit thought so or not, those chieftains might also have moved in to help liquidate Buono.

As Germain entered the police building he thought that of all the people in San Francisco this evening, or of all those including the City Attorney who would be in the city by midnight, Joe Buono, who thought himself secure — *probably* thought himself safe anyway — was the one most unlikely to see sunrise.

Sergeant Moore was in the corridor speaking to his bureau chief, Captain

Beaman, when Germain turned the corner from where the lift had deposited him. Beaman walked away before Moore, with some papers in his hand, looked up and saw who was approaching. He nodded and stepped inside the office, leaving the door open for Germain. He said, 'We've been in contact with Buchanan down in Sacramento trying to convince him to lie over down there until morning.'

Germain knew the rest of it from Moore's expression. 'He won't do it.'

The sergeant went behind his desk as the telephone rang. 'No. Not only won't he do it, but read this article from the evening paper.' He handed the thing to Germain as he reached for the telephone with his free hand.

The article was about the purpose and probable results of the conference the City Attorney had attended down at the Capitol. It was not only a cynical article, but it was also grumpily disapproving of Hale Buchanan, and ended with the comment that when the City Attorney arrived back in San Francisco on the midnight flight, the law-abiding people of the Bay Area would most assuredly be able to sleep more soundly knowing that Mr Buchanan, who used city funds for his junket, was back again to protect decent people from the villains and worse that made walking San Francisco's streets at night a frightening experience.

Germain tossed the paper on top of Moore's desk. He had read dozens of articles written in that vein; sometimes it seemed that columnists could not possibly see any good in public officials.

Moore put aside the telephone. 'Berryman,' he explained. 'I asked him to call me back if anything fresh turned up down in Sacramento. Well, Mr Buchanan has just refused to take an earlier flight back, which was Captain Beaman's suggestion. Berryman says our City Attorney is beginning to come across as some kind of cross between Joan of Arc and Abraham Lincoln. He's not going to be intimidated by the Cosa Nostra. He is also, Berryman said, keeping notes on this affair, so that when election time rolls around again he'll have something to show the voters.'

'Such as?' asked Germain.

Moore shrugged. 'I don't know. I suppose he'll detail it to the press how his indomitable courage, his great sagacity, and his sterling virtue, foiled the evil forces of the Mafia, and if the decent people of San Francisco want that kind of upstanding justice to prevail, they should re-elect him.' Moore sank down at the desk and tipped back. 'I don't think like a politician. Personally, when someone is out to hit me, I'm going to duck and dodge so hard they'll need a homing device on each bullet.' Moore smiled, something he did not do often. 'An hour ago I had a happy thought; when I get my vacation next October I think I'll go to Chicago and see if I can't dig up some nice, involved, messy murder to saddle *you* with.'

Germain's eyes twinkled. 'Come along any time. By the way, would it spoil your City Attorney's play if you asked the airline to delay their incoming flight from Sacramento at midnight, and you worked up a reasonable facsimile of Mr Buchanan in a flak-suit to arrive on an earlier flight? Something that might take the heat off; something that could induce Buono to make his play without hitting the right man?'

Sergeant Moore blew out a big breath and slowly shook his head. 'Strict orders through Captain Beaman from Mr Buchanan: The police are not to interfere except to the extent of making damned sure Joe Buono is grabbed before he can actually shoot.'

Germain's mouth dropped. 'How does anyone ever make damned sure an assassin won't succeed? I'm beginning to wonder about your City Attorney.'

Moore's telephone jangled again. He said his name into it, stared at the door a moment, then gave a crisp order. 'He's not going to use a rental car so concentrate on taxis . . . Okay; so the guy *looked* like Buono. It wasn't a positive identification, was it? Then stay on the taxis and don't worry too much about the rental outfits . . . The reason? John, this guy doesn't want anything left behind, including even fake identification, that might eventually tie him to a murder.

Taxis are about as anonymous as you can get and still have wheels under you . . . And John; make sure those checkers are on all the reservation counters at the airport.' Moore put the telephone down and shot to his feet. 'Care to man the battle-phone while I go get a cup of coffee?'

Germain did not mind at all, and although he worried a little because he didn't know what to say if someone called in for orders, as it turned out the telephone obliged him by not ringing until after Sergeant Moore returned, cup in hand.

Moore demonstrated an attribute that was invaluable in professional policemen, a variety of calm acceptance of conditions and events. He told Germain, between sips of black coffee, that time was running out on an early apprehension of Joe Buono. 'As soon as it's completely dark out I'm going to concentrate on a surround at the airport and forget about trying to nab him in the city.' Moore went to sit behind the desk again. 'In broad daylight, given enough time, I think we could find just about anyone. But this guy is a professional, daylight is running out, and we haven't really had enough time anyway.'

Germain was a professional too. 'Mario might make fair bait. Buono would recognize him.'

Moore nodded. 'The men watching Mario are old hands. They also have some of those pictures of Buono I had made and distributed. Mario is bait all right, but he also happens to be a walking bomb. If he sees Buono first we're going to have a disappointed City Attorney, aren't we?'

Germain was inclined to agree with Sergeant Moore about being an assassin's target. 'My personal, unofficial opinion about this Hale Buchanan, is that he's got to be an ego-maniac. No one in his right mind willingly risks getting shot just to win some votes.'

Moore finished his coffee. 'Don't they have to be ego-maniacs to make their life-work politics to begin with?'

The door opened and Captain Beaman walked in. He nodded at Germain, then shot a look at Sergeant Moore. 'Ron, the Commissioner, the mayor, and the State Attorney General are vitally interested in the Buchanan affair.'

Germain saw the dark shadow move swiftly across Sergeant Moore's face as he said, 'I'm not surprised that they are, Captain, but I hope it doesn't go any further, or the next thing we'll have newsmen swarming all over us.'

Beaman ran true to Germain's earlier appraisal of him by saying, 'Publicity doesn't hurt, providing it's the right kind.' Then, with that bit of philosophy dropped, he asked about progress and Moore was neither encouraging nor quite discouraging.

'It would help immensely, though,' he said, 'if the mayor could order Mr Buchanan to stay away until we've nailed the assassin.'

Captain Beaman slowly, but very firmly, shook his head from side to side. 'He couldn't make it stick. Well; I'll be at home and I'd like you to keep me informed.' Beaman nodded again at Germain and ducked out closing the door after himself.

Moore cocked a jaundiced eye, first at the door, then at Germain, but whatever his thoughts, and uncharitable though they obviously were, he said nothing.

Germain decided that keeping the vigil with Sergeant Moore was likely to prove more nerve-wracking than going out to the airport. He had never been a successful vigil-keeper. Some officers were best manning command-posts. Allan Germain was not one of them.

He made his excuses, which Sergeant Moore understood perfectly, and left the building in search of a taxi. He had to walk several hundred yards before finding an empty one, it being the busy time of evening for hacks, then he sat back and watched the city whip past in pastel, twilight colours. It looked like Chicago, or any other city Germain had ever seen, after sundown, and except for that tangy, rather refreshing sea-salt-scent, it could have been any other city.

17

Murder Number One!

The airport was swarming, as usual. A contingent of Asiatic air force officers had pre-empted one entire block of seats. Germain tried to make out their ranks but the pips had an arrangement that was unique in his experience.

A convention-aircraft had landed moments before Germain entered the upstairs lounge where passengers debarked. Cheerful people who looked rumpled from long hours of confinement aloft, poured through one of the landing-ramp doors.

Germain strolled through the various lounges, and although he did not definitely identify anyone who might have been an armed San Francisco detective, he was sure he had brushed arms with some of them. At least he *hoped* he had.

Once he thought he saw Mario Spina,

but it was only a glimpse in a moving crowd and Germain did not make any effort to verify it. For the time being Mario was safe from interception even though Germain, and Sergeant Moore also, evidently, did not believe Mario could lead the police to Joe Buono.

A South American airliner landed. Germain saw people surge forward in great numbers, among them dozens of newsmen with cameras. He heard the word 'hi-jacked' and had an explanation for all the excitement.

A number of arrivals and departures were called over a stereophonic loud-speaker system that was muted rather than loud and raspy.

Germain rode the mechanical path that conveyed people, like apples or cabbage, from one part of the building to another. It moved a little faster than a man could normally walk, and it left a person feeling a little foolish, standing in one place while the floor whisked them along.

He went out on to the lower-deck of the terminal building, where it was as bright as day, and went forth to stand, or rather to lean, upon the high causeway railing looking outward and downward where the private aeroplane area was.

Sergeant Moore would have those aeroplanes covered too. Joe Buono was going to walk into a lion's den that had only one way out again. As soon as he was inside, as soon as he made his assassination-attempt, that way out would be closed against him.

There were airport security men in uniform to back up the less identifiable undercover security men in plain clothes. Their perpetual headache was not psychopaths waiting to cause trouble in the building, it was psychopaths like defunct Foster Hellner planting explosive aboard airliners.

A man Germain recognized as the charter-pilot who had flown him to Angelo Scarpino's mountaintop came walking up the cement ramp from the private plane area. He looked freshly shaved and dressed. He also looked as thin-lipped and self-contained as ever. Germain waited until the man saw him, then nodded. The flyer studied Germain over the last twenty yards, then loosened, came over to lean upon the railing and light a cigarette as he said, 'Beautiful night.'

Germain, who had previously assessed this man as a tough, knowledgeable individual, agreed that it was indeed a beautiful night. He also asked, just to make conversation, how the charter-flight business was.

The ex-Marine pilot blew smoke. 'Better than driving a hack,' he said, 'and better than riding a tractor.' His grey eyes sparkled sardonically, 'but not as good as being a cop. No fringe benefits.'

Germain made no issue of the pilot's probe about Germain's occupation. 'To each his own,' he murmured, and the pilot nodded.

'Amen to that. And I guess it doesn't really make a whole lot of difference what a man does, if he lives long enough it will turn out to have been the wrong thing.' The charter-pilot got comfortable against the rail. 'You know, while I was sitting in that meadow with that goon keeping me from leaving the chopper, it occurred to me to ask for prisoner-pay.' The pilot's sardonic gaze lingered on Germain. 'I sat in there wondering whether I'd ferried in a gangster or a cop.'

'You know who is up there,' said Germain.

The pilot nodded. 'Yeah. By now everyone knows who's up there. Angelo Scarpino, the big-time Mafia leader. What I can't understand is why a guy who has all the money he's reputed to have, goes and sits on top of a lousy mountain.'

'Maybe he likes the lake, or the fresh air, or maybe just the isolation and the privacy.'

The pilot dropped his smoke and ground it out. 'You don't have to *live* in the mountains to appreciate them. Sometimes I toss some fishing gear into the chopper and fly in for a day of it. But that's enough. I've seen enough people who grew up in the mountains; they're 'squirrely' every one of 'em. If Scarpino sits up there long enough he'll get as squirrely as the others.' The pilot straightened up and cast another look upwards and around. There was a fresh

221

series of flashing landing-lights coming in over the arm of the bay. 'Now there is a good occupation,' he mused aloud, watching the giant aircraft let down. 'Thirty-five thousand dollars a year, free insurance, plenty of time off, free transportation any time.' He dropped his head as the huge aircraft settled out of sight upon the far side of the building. 'I guess there is one sure way of making certain you'll never be bothered by success — just be so damned indepen-dent you don't fit in.' He smiled and walked off towards the glass doors leading into the building. Germain watched him go. He was a rather handsome man in a rebellious way. Germain thought he would probably be a very interesting companion for a session of beer at a bar some evening.

This was not the evening though. Germain straightened up, glanced at his watch and let a number of people rush past into the building before he too started in that direction. A man built like a charter-pilot, that is, he was lean and rather tight-lipped and tanned, entered just ahead of Germain speaking quietly to the rather flashy blonde he was with. The man had a neat moustache, greying hair, and the popular kind of sideburns that did not go any lower than the bottom of the ears. He looked successful; his attire was in excellent taste and quality, and his bearing was confident. Germain thought that this man, whose back was to him as he entered the building perhaps fifteen feet in front of Germain, could have been used to exemplify the kind of people who were perfectly at home in airport lounges. The flashy blonde, well, she was just like a million other flashy blondes.

Germain hadn't got more than a glimpse of her face as she and her escort passed him outside, but he guessed she would look hardened and disillusioned. He knew the type.

The couple veered off, the man heading towards a lounge, the woman heading for a reservation counter, when Germain saw the small knot of people near the escalator leading to the upstairs observation lounge. He forgot about the flashy blonde and her companion when three converging men he identified immediately as plain-clothes men came out of the crowd and converged. Germain hastened forward.

Uniformed guards appeared to direct the onlookers about their business, and most of them went without much urging. Germain was stopped too, but he produced his I.D. folder and although the guard looked doubtful, he allowed Germain through.

The man lying crumpled at the foot of the escalator was no heart-attack victim, as one of the guards was saying to the onlookers he was seeking to disperse. Germain saw the scarlet pool spreading beneath the man as the plain-clothes men moved him.

It was the tough-eyed, independent helicopter pilot.

Germain would have stooped closer but the airport people lifted the body and whisked it to the nearest private office. Evidently they were experienced at this sort of thing, and evidently, too, there were rules about getting injured people out of public view as swiftly as possible.

At the door of the room where they took the helicopter pilot a city detective stopped Germain, and this time the resistance was more determined. Even the I.D. folder did not make the detective relent.

'Sorry,' growled the detective. 'We don't need outside help, Inspector.'

Germain pocketed the folder. 'I've been working with Sergeant Ronald Moore of homicide,' said Germain. 'I'm part of the stakeout tonight.'

The detective relented, but without any enthusiasm. He allowed Germain to enter the room, which was some kind of very tidy storage compartment, large and lighted, with shelves of supplies on both sidewalls. A burly detective glanced up from looking through a wallet as Germain entered. The detective saw the way Germain stared, and shrugged. 'He's dead.'

It was true. What was more, the charter-pilot had been hit squarely between the shoulder-blades from the rear and probably had no warning at all. One moment his heart had been pumping, the next moment it had been burst by a bullet. He died while falling.

The detective with the wallet asked who Germain was, got a glimpse of the Chicago Police Department I.D. folder, and nodded. 'Yeah. You're the man who has been working with Sergeant Moore. Well, I've sent him word we've got a murder out here — only it sure doesn't fit with anything I was told. Do you know this dead man?'

Germain said, 'I knew him. He flew me up-country this morning.'

The detective closed the dead pilot's wallet and gazed down where two other officers were making a minute search. 'Maybe there's some connection, then,' he muttered.

Germain dropped to one knee and examined the wound. There was no scorch. He stood up and said, 'Anyone hear the shot?'

No one had, and the burly detective put Germain's suspicion into words.

'Silencer. It's old-fashioned, going around making noise any more.' A younger man entered the room and the burly detective raised thick brows at him. The younger man said, 'Sergeant Moore's on his way.'

'That's all?' growled the burly detective. 'What about the meat wagon?'

'He said he'd take care of that, and the lab men,' replied the younger detective.

Germain stood a moment longer, trying to make some kind of sense out of what looked to him like a perfectly pointless killing, then he went back outside, saw a man with sawdust and a mop scrubbing out the red stain at the foot of the escalator as people eddied around him, unconcerned, and thought that it did not take very long, a couple of minutes, to wipe out a life and remove whatever final marks were left over to show where it had been snuffed out.

He looked round as the officer at the door asked if the victim was dead. 'Yeah. He was probably dead before he hit the floor,' said Germain, and strolled out a dozen or so yards to a bench where he sat and proceeded to fill his pipe.

Something was rattling around inside his head. He lit up, sat back to keep an eye on the supply-room door until Sergeant Moore arrived, and when the idea settled down where it made sense, he sat like a statue allowing the fired-up pipe to grow cold between his teeth.

The charter-pilot had the same build, the same general appearance, even the same tough-hard expression Joe Buono had! If someone had glimpsed him walking past towards that escalator, in a crowd and not in the best light, he could very easily have mistaken him for Buono. Especially if he were keyed up and crawling with anxiety.

Mario Spina!

Germain emptied the pipe, dropped it into a pocket and arose. Sergeant Moore was striding forward through the thinning drift of people also heading in the general direction of the escalator. Germain moved to intercept him before he reached the supply-room door.

Moore halted at sight of Germain, looking anxious and harassed. He made no greeting and offered no smile as he said, 'What happened?'

'The helicopter pilot who flew me to Scarpino's place this morning,' replied Germain. 'One bullet in the back. Killed him instantly. Sergeant, when you look at that corpse think back to the picture and description of Joe Buono.'

'Similar?'

'Almost identical. It never occurred to me until I saw the corpse lying out on the floor in there.'

Moore scowled. 'Mario?'

Germain nodded. 'That would be my guess. Maybe we'd better not let our bait wander around any longer. You were right; he's an ambulatory bomb. If it occurs to him that he iced the wrong man, he'll probably try again.'

Moore said, 'Yeah, Inspector, and if he happens to see you wandering around in here you'll be next. Okay, I'll radio the surveillance team to pick him up.' Moore walked on over to the supply-room door and was passed through by the detective standing guard over there.

Germain had been too engrossed in the murder to consider his own position, but now he did, slowly turning to range a searching gaze among the people moving on all sides of him. Not only was Moore correct, but if Mario was hovering nearby — which he probably wasn't but there were no guarantees about that — he just might try for another victim.

Germain unbuttoned his coat. He felt nakedly exposed despite the number of people moving past in both directions. It was not the first time he'd felt that way, but regardless of the number of times a man felt as though he were being measured for death, the same cold eeriness prevailed.

18

The Time Passes

As discreet as the morgue people were at removing the corpse, what really kept onlookers from showing much interest was that people in the airport were too engrossed with their own affairs, their own problems, to pay much attention to a wheeled-stretcher being whisked from the building.

Otherwise, those uniformed guards as well as the plainclothes men dispersed briskly in all directions and only that stoic swamper who had cleaned up the puddle at the foot of the escalator was left, to clean up the second puddle on the floor of the supply-room.

Sergeant Moore joined Allan Germain and said, 'Well, it's after ten o'clock which means we've got less than two hours to secure this damned place.' He turned as a detective Germain had never seen before detached himself from the crowd and said something briskly, then waited. Moore swore, which surprised Germain, whose impression had been that nothing could ever really ruffle Sergeant Moore. But after Moore sent the detective off and turned, Germain understood the sergeant's mood.

'Mario got away from his surveillance team.' Moore looked more disgusted than angry. 'How does that grab you? Those men are some of the best in the department, and Mario — well — Mario's a ferret and nothing else.'

Germain made an excuse for the officers. 'In this building, at night, you could lose an elephant, for a little while.'

Moore was not to be placated. 'They'd better find him fast or I know a couple of guys who'll be emptying their upstairs desks by Monday morning.' Then Sergeant Moore shelved that to say, 'This should be routine. The building is sealed off. They'll pick Mario up, I'm confident of that. If he thinks he hit Buono he'll be trying to get out of here, and even if he makes it, there is another team on his car. But what about Buono? Aside from a couple of pretty good leads in the city, which were hours old when I finally got them, that damned man is more elusive than a ghost.'

Germain's explanation to this dilemma was reasonable. 'He's one of their best killers. He's been at his trade a long time. No one is going to walk up and tap him on the shoulder. You know that, Sergeant.'

Moore grunted. 'Yeah. And I know something else too. The mayor and the Police Commissioner, and the Attorney General are all sitting with poised pencils waiting to send a memo down to Captain Beaman if I blow this assignment.'

That same younger officer who had appeared before, returned to murmur to Sergeant Moore and Germain, who was watching, saw Moore's face brighten. The sergeant turned. 'They've picked Mario up again. He's heading for his car let's go.'

The young officer remained behind but Germain went off briskly with Sergeant Moore. Evidently Mario had got out of the building before someone outside, with a walkie-talkie, had passed the word. As they trotted down the front causeway in the direction of the parking area, Germain suggested that Mario was not as important as Buono, and Moore had a brusque answer to that.

'Buono isn't going to warm up for another hour. We've got time for this little job.'

A plain-clothes man detached himself from among some parked cars at their approach, peered closely, then pointed the way. He had a transceiver in his other hand. Sergeant Moore did not stop and the plain-clothes man did not say anything that would cause him to do so.

The parking area at San Francisco Airport, aside from a multi-decked cement building, also covered a rather vast macadamized area. Some of the rows of cars Germain passed had dust on them as though they'd been in their places for perhaps as long as a week. It would have been a most excellent source of tyres, wheels, radios and so forth, for enterprising thieves except that it was lighted, patrolled, and was also under the surveillance of men in the towers atop of the main building.

Germain saw three men, fanned out and facing forward, before Moore saw them, and said something that made Moore slacken pace. One of those detectives was speaking into a small transceiver with the shiny aerial sticking straight up beside his head. He was farthest off. Another detective turned, studied the pair of approaching men, then must have recognized Sergeant Moore because he waved him on in with an upraised arm, and when they were closer, the detective said, 'Over three lanes. The team that's covering him is calling in. He's only a short distance from the car.'

Moore nodded, did not reply, and jerked his head at Allan Germain. They went more slowly and carefully from here on. When it was possible to pick out the Continental, Germain showed it to Moore, then the pair of them halted as a lumpy silhouette moved furtively among the cars heading in the Continental's direction.

Germain expected Moore to advocate moving closer, but Moore stood where he was, waiting and watching.

Mario moved in fits and starts. He was concentrating more on what lay behind him than he was on the car. Germain felt a kind of casual interest and comfortable detachment. Whatever else was about to happen, there was little chance of Mario using Germain for a target.

Finally, Mario got up beside the Continental, cast a quick, triumphant look all around, opened the door and slid in behind the wheel. Moore stood like stone. It was not possible to see into the darkened car very well, but Mario was visible, head and shoulders. He was sitting motionless.

Moore sighed. 'Let's go,' he said, and walked ahead.

Germain did not see the man whose snub-nosed revolver was pressing icily into Mario's neck from behind until they were within only a few feet of the car. Also, on the opposite side, a large man was getting out of an adjacent car.

Moore reached, opened the door and

jerked his head at Mario. No one said a word as Mario climbed out looking wilted. The officer who had been lying down behind the back of the front seat stood up to his full height, and Germain wondered how he'd ever been able to crouch back there. The officer put up his service weapon and tried to smooth his rumpled jacket and trousers as four men converged.

Moore motioned for Mario to turn, to put his hands atop the Continental. Mario obeyed, still totally silent. One of the surveillance men frisked him, lifted away the long-barrelled Police Positive revolver with the sinister black tube screwed to the front of the barrel, and as Moore took the thing he looked at Germain, breaking the silence.

'They keep turning up, these old-issue weapons.' He allowed Germain to examine the gun. Germain was more interested in the lumpy man who had been carrying the gun. As Mario was swung forward, both arms hauled behind him for the cuffs, Germain said, 'Bad trip, Mario. You hit an innocent man.'

Mario looked tired and distraught but he managed to be defiant. 'I didn't hit anyone. I don't know what you guys are swarming around me for.'

Germain said it again. 'You killed the charter-pilot who flew us to Scarpino's place this morning.'

They all saw Mario stiffen. It came over Germain what had happened: Mario, seeing a man who resembled Joe Buono, and confident he knew that build and appearance, had made a terrible, but understandable, mistake; he had killed someone he remembered seeing, not someone he thought he knew. What Moore had said was true, Mario was out of his league in this kind of an affair. He was the kind of man who could kill any victim who was specifically pointed out to him, but if there was any doubt, or any strong resemblance, Mario could be trusted to use a gun against the wrong man.

Sergeant Moore said, 'What did you learn about Buono at the garage, Mario?'

'What garage?' Mario glared. 'Okay

. . . I learnt nothing. No one's seen Joe. Are you sure it was the charter pilot, Germain?'

Moore nodded, so did Germain, so did two of the other officers. Mario then denied that he'd shot anyone, and Moore held up the gun to drop out the cylinder and examine the casings. 'One empty shell,' he said, flicked the cylinder back into place and handed the weapon to another detective. 'For the last time, Mario — what have you picked up about Buono?'

Mario's reply was convincing. 'Nothing, not a damned thing. And you won't either.' Mario knew he was caught, and caught hard, but evidently he also had contempt for the legal processes because he said, 'And you won't make this bum roust stick either. I'll send word to Mr Scarpino. I'll be out by morning.'

Sergeant Moore did not dispute this although he safely could have; an ex-felon on bail pending arraignment for aiding a fugitive, carrying a gun, shooting someone to death, was well beyond the tolerance of influence even though Angelo

239

Scarpino pulled every string at his disposal. Mario was going to jail, and this time he would not be allowed to post bond.

Sergeant Moore jerked his head. The pair of officers who had been Mario Spina's surveillance team, turned and took the prisoner away with them. Mario said nothing, but he put a particularly venomous glare upon Allan Germain.

Moore wasn't very concerned about that, and neither was Germain. An officer carrying one of the little palm-sized transceivers came up to say Sergeant Moore was wanted inside the front entrance to the building. Germain started back again, his long legs having no difficulty keeping up with Sergeant Moore. 'I'll guess,' he said to Moore. 'Your people on the reservation counters have found someone.'

Moore was cynical. 'Or else they're waiting to tell me they haven't found anything at all.'

It was Sergeant Moore who turned out to be correct. He and Germain barely cleared the swinging glass doors before that alert, clear-eyed young detective who had been acting as Moore's liaison contact, came forth to say that although the officers covering the passenger desk had come up with some names which they'd telephoned in to have processed by the Indentification Computer, they did not believe they had any lead on Joe Buono at all. Moore looked almost triumphantly at Germain. 'What did I tell you? For stolen hub-caps, cameras, even poodle dogs and calico cats, you can depend upon the San Francisco Police Department to deliver, but a professional assassin can run through the whole damned city dressed in a red-white-and-blue suit, and we'll never even see him.' He turned back to the younger officer. 'Tell Mallory to check the private flight-line, and also ask him to hurry up with that damned taxi-check.'

The youthful officer hiked away very briskly and Sergeant Moore watched his departure with a wagging head. Germain felt like smiling. The more conditions piled up adversely the more glum and dour and fast-thinking Sergeant Moore got; Germain's original syllepsis had not been wrong after all.

Moore held up his arm for Germain to see the hands of his wristwatch. 'Three-quarters of an hour,' said the Sergeant, 'and about sixty cops falling over each other around here, and I'll lay you a bet we go right down to the line with this — and maybe then we fall flat too.'

'The City Attorney must not think you'll fall flat,' responded Germain. 'It's his neck that'll be on the line before the hour is out.'

'And mine,' growled Moore. 'And yours. And everyone else's who's on the lousy assignment with us.' He stood a moment, then raised a frowning face. 'Suppose Buono doesn't make the attempt tonight? I mean, if there's no hint of him anywhere around, including the flight desks, maybe he's decided to try Buchanan's residence, or maybe the courthouse entrance tomorrow morning.'

Germain countered that question with one of his own. 'Do you have men guarding his residence?'

Moore looked weary. 'Yeah. And the

242

courthouse. And the county garage where he leaves his car each morning. And his own car, which was parked in the basement of the building across the way. I've got his itinerary, and there is a man to protect him from the second he steps off his lousy airliner tonight, until he gets up to brush his teeth in the morning, and from there throughout his whole blessed day and back to bed again. Buono may not know it, but the only way he'll manage a successful hit against Hale Buchanan will be during those little split-second intervals when Buchanan walks from his front door to his garage, or when he leaves his car in the county garage and walks to the courthouse lift. Germain, he makes Buchanan tonight, or he's going to go up against impossible odds later on.'

A bushy-headed young man carrying a guitar case and wearing exaggerated sunglasses after eleven o'clock at night walked up and asked directions to the local helicopter-ferry pad that carried people from the airport to any one of the many rooftops in downtown San

Francisco. Moore glared and turned his back. The young man accepted this overt hostility without a murmur and went in search of another source of guidance.

Germain fished forth his pipe, glanced at his wristwatch, stoked the pipe and fired up. Whatever happened had to happen very soon now. For the first time in several hours when an arrival or a departure was announced over the loud-speakers Germain paid attention. He wondered if, by any chance, the City Attorney's flight could be ahead of schedule. He did not mention this to Sergeant Moore, and not entirely because two detectives came up to confer in low tones, excluding everyone but Sergeant Moore from whatever it was they had to report.

19

The New Joe Buono

Sergeant Moore was functioning under tension, but as Germain knew, it was not the first time, nor would it be the last time. Whatever those two detectives had come up to tell him did not seem to add anything to his burden even though they conferred so quietly that Germain could hear none of what they said, and after he'd sent them away, Moore turned and shrugged. 'Did you ever wonder,' he asked, 'what would happen if a round-the-clock tight surveillance was kept on a big-city air terminal just for the hell of it?'

Germain caught the drift of this. 'What's turned up?'

'A heroin middleman we've been looking for,' replied Moore, showing no enthusiasm. 'They plucked him off his flight. The computer that was filtering passengers detected him — but nothing on Joe Buono.'

'Suppose,' suggested Germain, 'you had the public address system announced that Mr Angelo Scarpino was wanted at the reservation desk for his flight.'

Moore looked briefly blank, then said, 'Buono would never take that kind of bait.'

Germain was not convinced his suggestion was all that bad, but he did not push it. He and Sergeant Moore went to the nearest restaurant for coffee. A man in a dark suit at a rear table nodded and Moore nodded back.

Germain looked at his watch without letting Moore see him do it. Sometimes the time sped and at other times it barely crawled. When their coffee arrived Moore gazed around the room before drinking. The restaurant had an air of frenetic activity even, as now, when it wasn't terribly busy. The people who killed time there did not do so as most people would have; even when they acted relaxed they were constantly referring to either the large dial-clock on the wall, or their own watches.

Germain saw that alert, youthful detective approaching and sighed inwardly. Moore's liaison people were like leeches; even when the sergeant went off to sit for five minutes, they were on duty. Of course that was a good thing, but it also happened to be irritating.

The youthful officer leaned, said something, then straightened up, waiting. Moore looked across the table, 'They finally have something,' he said, shoving back from the table. 'It's probably a dud but let's check it out.'

For Germain the hike back into the central area where those long rows of reservation counters stood, was like walking a treadmill that he'd walked before, but when they arrived where a detective stood conversing with a young man in a white jacket with his employer's airline insignia over the right-hand pocket, Germain's interest quickened.

The detective wasted no time. He showed Sergeant Moore and Inspector Germain a passenger-tally. One name had been underscored in red. 'Mr and Mrs James Belton of San Francisco *en route* to Salt Lake City, Utah.'

Moore and Germain looked up. The detective picked up a piece of airline-monogrammed note paper upon which someone had written a message in a very heavy hand. 'It's customary for reservation clerks to get an address and a telephone number.'

The man in the white jacket explained. 'In case there's a last-minute delay, or perhaps a cancellation.'

Germain knew all this. So, presumably, did Sergeant Moore, who said, being so polite it was painful, 'All right. Let's have it. Mr Belton gave you a phony address?'

The clerk looked at the big detective, who nodded at Moore. 'Address *and* telephone number. The address is of a rooming-house and the telephone number is of a third-rate downtown hotel.'

Sergeant Moore took the paper and without a word swung a nearby telephone towards himself atop the reservation counter and dialled. The others watched.

When he completed the call he looked at Germain and softly said, 'Bingo!' He smiled. 'Earlier this afternoon it was reported that a desk-clerk had made a positive identification of Buono.' Moore patted the telephone fondly. 'That was the same hotel.'

Germain stepped closer, read the name 'Mr and Mrs James Belton' from the passenger list, scanned the flight number on the list, then looked back towards the schedule upon the wall behind the reservation counter. 'Flight Nine to Salt Lake City leaving at twelve-fifteen.' The reservation-clerk took his cue from this, went back behind his counter and deliberated a moment over some teletype messages.

'On time,' he informed the detectives, 'at the last report. It will be coming north from San Diego and Los Angeles. Arrival here will be midnight, on the dot, departure will be twelve-fifteen tonight.'

Moore asked about luggage. The clerk stepped through a door behind his counter, peered, then beckoned. All three detectives went back there into the baggage room, where a youthful attendant was reading a physics book and eating a banana while sitting on someone's upended suitcase. He jumped when three large men barged in. The clerk showed them the baggage of Mr and Mrs James Belton, while the collegeboy baggage-man seemed anxious to hide what had looked like loafing on the job, and went to pull those two bags over where Moore and Germain, and the other detective could get at them.

Moore said, 'Too bad; no warrant,' and gazed calmly at Germain, then he jerked his head to lead the way back out of the baggage room and around in front of the counter where he addressed the big detective. 'Mallory, set it up. They'll be summoned to the counter on a reservation foul-up. Have a man at each end of the counter and pass the word to tighten up all around.' As the big detective moved off Moore told the reservation-clerk what he wanted, and the look he got made Germain smile. Germain stepped behind the counter and held out a hand. 'Lend me your jacket. All you've got to do is make the announcement over the P.A. system, then duck into the baggage room.'

The clerk liked this idea much better. His coat fitted Germain, a much larger man, only because those coats were loose-fitting by design so that they would be interchangeable among airline employees. While Germain was making the exchange the clerk made his announcement. Sergeant Moore told him to repeat it, then Moore winked at Germain and went across to a bench near the far wall, picked up an abandoned newspaper, crossed his legs and started reading.

The clerk did his part and disappeared into the luggage room, and at once a complication rose. Three people approached the counter wanting reservations. Germain had to summon a reluctant clerk to take care of them. He did it by keeping one eye on everyone who seemed about to approach the counter and as soon as he'd completed the paperwork, he ducked back into the rear room again.

Germain leaned on the counter looking

every inch the bored reservation-clerk. It was getting close to midnight; most of the ebullience, the noise and normal activity of the terminal, was down to low-key. Even the people who had slept most of the day in anticipation of being awake for the late flights, did not look very brighteyed.

Germain leaned and watched, and waited. He had picked out the converging detectives, or thought he had, but that was all. People strolled past by the dozen. Germain watched them too, as did Sergeant Moore and the stake-out men. Buono, the professional, might approach the counter without hesitation, but it was more likely if he came at all that he would first reconnoitre. Another time he might not, but this was not another time; this was the night he was to murder a prominent man. He would be as wary as a hunting wolf.

Moore put aside the newspaper and consulted his watch just as a voluptuous woman with silvery-blonde hair approached the counter. Germain, watching Moore's action, saw the woman from the edge of his eye. He had two thoughts that were almost simultaneous. The first one was that someone else wanted a reservation and he'd have to drag the reluctant clerk back from the luggage room. The second thought was that he had seen this woman before. She was a flashy blonde with a hard, old-young face.

He remembered her just as she reached the counter. He also remembered the lean, athletic man who had been with her. They had preceded him into the building more than an hour earlier. As the woman looked up Germain was poised to nod at Moore. He held off until after the woman spoke.

'I'm Mrs Belton,' she said. 'You paged me?'

Germain smiled, looked over her shoulder and nodded. Sergeant Moore sat perfectly still. No one approached the counter while the woman was there. Germain asked to see Mr Belton's tickets and made a show of comparing them with a passenger list below the counter. 'It seems,' he said, 'that these two seats were previously sold down in Los Angeles, Mrs Belton, and our problem now is to confirm that they belong to you and your husband.'

The flashy blonde woman began to scowl at Germain. 'Well, we paid good money for those seats,' she said, 'and we're on a schedule.'

Germain slid the tickets back into their little envelope and passed them back across the counter with a reassuring smile. 'Don't worry, I'll call Los Angeles immediately and confirm your reservations. It was *their* error, not ours at this end. You will have your reservations, and the airline is very sorry to have put you to any inconvenience.'

The flashy blonde looked reassured. 'You are quite positive?'

Germain said, 'Quite positive. Thank you for answering the call, Mrs Belton.' He kept his smile up as the woman put the envelope back into her handbag and turned away. Then he nodded again, and finally Sergeant Moore moved; he did not leave the bench though, he simply turned and gazed impassively after Mrs Belton. It was another man, farther along, who moved. He turned to walk ahead of the flashy blonde and for some little distance he kept his lead without looking back, then he veered off at a car-rental counter and engaged another rather tall man behind the counter in conversation, handed over what appeared to be a car-key, and with the flashy blonde something like twenty or thirty feet ahead walking in the direction of the escalator, he walked off in the same direction.

Germain continued to lean on the reservation counter until Sergeant Moore stood up, yawned, and nodded. Then Germain jettisoned his airline jacket, poked his head into the baggage room to call the 'all-clear' and scooped up his own coat as he stepped out from behind the counter to join Moore in walking towards the distant escalator.

Moore said, 'Upstairs, apparently, and I'll say one thing for your boy — he's smart. I was expecting a lone individual.'

'You don't know *how* smart,' stated Germain. 'I saw him enter the building not very long after I first arrived out here with that woman. He walked right past me wearing a neat moustache and his hair was grey over the ears, with sideburns. I thought at the time he was probably some kind of successful businessman who liked his women well-upholstered.'

Sergeant Moore shot Germain a look. 'Your own man and you didn't recognize him?'

Germain didn't try an alibi, he just kept walking. It happened every day and Sergeant Moore damned well knew it.

They were approaching the escalator when the tall officer who had been tailing the flashy blonde appeared at the upstairs railing looking down. Moore, who evidently knew this man well, glanced up as he preceded Germain on to the escalator along with dozens of other people, and sighed. 'Something went wrong,' he muttered.

When they arrived upstairs the detective confirmed Moore's telepathy by nodding in the direction of a mahogany door that said, 'Ladies,' looking very disgusted.

Germain strolled away leaving Moore

to keep the vigil with the other detective. He had in mind strolling through the upstairs lounges in search of the man with greying hair and neat little moustache.

People in the first lounge were queueing up near a ramp where a uniformed attendant manned a velvet-covered rope. Germain looked at the line of faces but without any hope at all; Buono was not going to fly out of San Francisco before he made his strike.

He went through three other lounges and out into the wide, well-lighted walkway beyond. People milled like sheep, some bewildered, some trying to act very blasé — these were usually the young ones — and here and there little teary-eyed groups stood huddled around someone who was evidently about to depart from the bosom of the family.

But he did not see the well-dressed, successful-looking man with the greying hair and moustache. He pondered a moment; Buono would perhaps not suspect anything, even yet, but the man was not going to run any unnecessary risks either. In his shoes, Germain would not have remained long in one place where later on, after the murder, someone might remember what he looked like.

The only place in a building as crowded as an airport terminal where a man could wait for an hour or so to kill someone, without attracting even any casual attention, would be a rest-room.

Germain stood out in the wide corridor looking around until he saw the first door marked 'Men'. It occurred to him that there would probably be at least a dozen such rest-rooms throughout the building. Instead of starting a search he headed back to the place where he had left Sergeant Moore to suggest that a man be detailed to each rest-room with the fresh description of Joe Buono.

It was fifteen minutes to midnight when he started back.

20

The Last Quarter-Hour

Sergeant Moore listened to Germain's suggestion and heeded it by sending the man who had been trailing the flashy blonde in search of Detective Mallory, who would implement it. Then Moore and Germain moved off a short distance where a display-window reflected the ghostly outline of the door beyond which the flashy blonde had disappeared. Moore said it was getting too close to blast-off time, and if they didn't find Buono soon, he was going to shorten his lines, meaning he was going to bring in his outside men and put a wall of detectives around the disembarking lounge where the City Attorney would enter the building.

Germain was gazing at the display in front of him when he saw the ghostly reflection of the door move. He watched.

The woman who came forth was not the flashy blonde. Germain sighed. 'This kind of thing could give a man ulcers.'

Moore snorted. 'And you're from Chicago,' he muttered. 'Me, I've got to put in another seven years before I can retire. How will it look on my record if I fumbled an attempt to scotch an assassination attempt of a City Attorney?'

Germain, who knew Hale Buchanan only by reputation, said 'Maybe he'll have a blue funk. I've seen it happen. They are brave as all hell right up until it's time to stand up, then it all oozes out through the bottoms of their boots.'

'Not this time,' replied Moore, turning his head to glance around as he spoke. 'Not Buchanan. There have been times when he's annoyed the hell out of me, but I'll give him this much; he's no coward.'

'Just foolish, then,' muttered Germain, and saw the reflection of the door move again. This time it was the flashy blonde.

Germain sighed. 'I was beginning to think someone had slipped a clutch of eggs under her.'

They waited until the blonde was

heading across, on an angle, towards the lounge that would accommodate her twelve-fifteen o'clock flight, then strolled after her as though they too were to board the same aeroplane.

The blonde neither looked back, nor to her left or right. Germain admired the purposefulness of her behaviour. She looked as unconcerned as it was possible to look. Even when she entered the large, spacious lounge and sought a seat, she acted perfectly at ease.

She had good reason to act that way; the people on either side of her were, neither of them, the athletic man with the greying hair and moustache. Sergeant Moore grunted his disgust, but Germain, his hopes pinned upon the rest-rooms, was not very disappointed. As he pointed out when they strolled on through, whatever preparations Joe Buono had to make, would have to be made about now. Sergeant Moore looked up, pained.

'Thanks,' he growled. 'You're sure an encouraging cuss.'

Where Moore encountered one of his plain-clothes men, he passed an order that the flashy blonde was to be kept under constant watch. He said he would send up another man, then he and Germain went along to the nearly empty lounge where the City Attorney would disembark, and Moore detached one of his men from that area to go back where the blonde was. He told this officer that if anyone who even faintly resembled Joe Buono appeared anywhere near that woman, he was to be arrested at once. He also said that if no one approached the blonde, as soon as the City Attorney's flight came in, the woman was to be taken into custody and held downstairs at the central information desk until Moore himself came to talk to her.

The detective named Mallory came up and offered Moore a slip of paper, and a wry comment. 'Nice invention, those computers. Now we've got the cab number and the time when it brought this man and his blonde woman out here.'

Moore no more than glanced at the message from headquarters. 'Everything seems to be obsessed with perfect hindsight tonight,' he growled, and balled up the message and pitched it into a large urn nearby.

The public address system announced that the midnight flight from Portland, Oregon, would be arriving, southbound, within the next few minutes. Moore glanced at his watch and Germain turned towards the velvet-covered rope that kept people off the disembarking ramp; a young, dark man in the cap and jacket of an airline official, was taking up his position over there. Very shortly now, the City Attorney's flight would arrive. Each time the public address system announced a touch-down or an imminent touch-down, Germain held his breath.

Moore went to stand by a huge, thick window gazing outward where mercury lamps and brighter, whiter, lamps, bathed the miles of landing area in brilliance. As Germain came over the sergeant said, 'Eleven men downstairs on the ramp or on the flight-line. Seven more on the mezzanine. Six up here, three more on the roof with rifles and scopes, and Berryman is with his nibs, plus you and me. He turned as Mallory came over and said something about the rest-rooms.

'No one in any of them answering Buono's description, Sergeant.'

Moore frowned. 'He's not invisible.'

Mallory's heavy features showed not the faintest hint of humour as he said, 'Maybe he is; if he's in this building most of us must have seen him at least once. But where?'

Moore was not in the mood for this, so all he said by way of reply was: 'Keep them moving, keep looking, he's somewhere around and we've got a few minutes left to find him.'

Mallory moved off without any change of expression. Germain hardly noticed. If, he told himself, Joe Buono had planned this murder at midnight as well as it seemed that he had, disguising himself and picking up a flashy blonde somewhere to add to his deception, all on the basis of what he *didn't* know — that the airport building was crawling with police — then what would his reaction have been if he had known he was being sought by nearly two dozen homicide detectives?

The answer, Germain thought, was that Buono would not have made the murder-attempt. He was not a zealot, he was instead a coldly practical professional killer, who went about his business as calmly as a professional plumber or carpenter.

It occurred to Germain that perhaps Buono *did* know something, or suspected something; perhaps the reason no one could find him was because he was not in the building.

That thought gave Germain a hot flash. He turned and said, 'When Buono iced that bomb-nut back in Chicago, the nut had a pair of airline coveralls, the kind maintenance men wear.'

Moore thought on that a moment, then nodded. 'Okay; go down there if you'd like — if you're thinking what I'm thinking. I'll detail a man.' Moore looked a little wan. 'I've got a bad feeling about this situation. By now, on every other stakeout I've ever been on, we'd either have got him or would have him where we could watch him.'

Germain left, moving fast because time was ticking away. It did not take long to get downstairs and out on to the tarmac, but he was stopped almost at once by an airline security guard. Mallory saved him, moving in from a different direction. The guard backed off and stone-faced Detective Mallory asked what Germain was up to. After hearing the explanation he pointed out the area containing the office of the maintenance crews. While he was doing this a young, somewhat scarred but pleasant detective walked up. His name was Jim Madison and he was the man assigned to Germain by Sergeant Moore.

Germain sent him to the maintenance office to ascertain from the supervisor, or foreman, whoever was in charge, that the crew which would board the aeroplane on Flight 9 was in full strength with no last-minute personnel substitutions, and that he would know each man by sight.

Mallory listened, did not act very impressed, and eventually Mallory went hiking for the stairway to continue his endless prowling. As Sergeant Moore's liaison throughout the building, from tarmac-level to the rooftop, Mallory was getting his share of exercise.

A huge silver airliner bumped away from the loading ramp looking ungainly and too large to fly. Germain went out where work crews were trundling back the ramp and a caterers' lorry that had victualled the aircraft, and where a fuel-truck was making a careful turn in the confusion to also get back near the building. Germain guessed that this was an overseas flight. The aeroplane was very obviously heavily laden with fuel and passengers.

He stood in the shadow of an immense cement and steel piling, part of the underpinning of the terminal building, studying faces. The only time it was difficult to see them clearly was when the maintenance crewmen moved back close enough to the building so that their features were night-shadowed. It was an easy matter to overlook about a third of the workmen; they were negroes. The other two-thirds consisted of general technicians; a stranger bluffing his way among them would never be able to make it. Those men worked fast and efficiently; every one of them knew exactly what to do.

Still, Germain thought his hunch might pay off. After all — and this must have impressed Joe Buono — that bomb-nut back in Chicago had worked out the best of all ways to reach an airliner, and by now it was highly probable to Germain that Joe Buono was not in the building, so, unless he had abandoned his scheme, he would be *outside* the building. Germain hoped he was wrong; he hoped Buono had decided not to hit the City Attorney at the airport, and except for one thing, Germain might have liked that idea: The blonde upstairs and the *pair* of airline reservations.

Of course that, too, could have been a ruse, a deliberate plant to throw any watchers or searchers off balance. But only, thought Germain, providing Joe Buono knew he was in danger, and everything the police had done thus far was based on the premise that Buono did *not* know.

Two maintenance men strolled over near where Germain lounged, lit up, gazed out where the waiting airliner squatted, and one said, 'Ten minutes, one more off-loading, and quitting time. C'mon down to the tavern and I'll buy tonight.'

The second man grunted. 'You know better. Tonight's payday and my old woman'll be sitting up watching the late show on television, waiting for me like a hungry eagle.'

That big airliner out on the runway got clearance and ran up its whistling turbines. That ended all conversation for a while. It almost ended all thought. Germain turned as the detective who had been assigned to him came up with a negative headshake, leaned and yelled: 'Nothing. No substitutions. The whole crew is working.'

Germain turned back to watching the airliner waddle ahead. He hadn't been too hopeful, nor had he thought Joe Buono would actually get that involved. Like the bomb-nut back in Chicago, it wasn't necessary to actually *join* a maintenance crew. As long as a man had the right kind of coveralls he could get out to the airliner, and getting too involved, trying too hard to act a part, would show him up to the experienced maintenance men.

The airliner lurched ahead, very much like a fledgling goose. Like all giant aircraft it did not look right when earthbound. It spewed a sooty stream of exhaust and suddenly reared its round nose into the air. A few yards more and it was airborne. Then, finally, it was in its own environment. Climbing, chewing up great yards of illuminated space, it went for altitude. When it shot past the ground-brilliance the whistling whine lessened.

Germain's companion, Jim Madison, glanced around where crewmen were making ready for the next arrival or departure, and sighed loudly enough for it to be audible. 'I'd be on the roof with a telescopic sight,' he said, then seemed to reconsider. 'Maybe not; Mallory said that's staked out too.'

Germain explained why he thought Buono would try for Hale Buchanan down where they stood, and mid-way through this explanation the public address system announced the incoming flight from Southern California, by way of several San Joaquin Valley cities — and Sacramento.

That was Hale Buchanan's flight.

Madison listened, craned his neck to scan the dark southward sky, saw nothing and said, 'I think I'd have leaned on the blonde a little instead of trying to play this lousy affair right down to the line, by ear.'

Germain, mildly annoyed by his companion's breeziness, said ironically. 'Would you? Suppose she's sitting up there as Buono's decoy? The minute you approached her he'd guess who you were.'

'Maybe she's not his decoy, though.'

'And maybe,' retorted Germain, 'this isn't the flight coming in, but I have as much respect for the accuracy of the airline people as I have for Joe Buono's ability to bring off a business-like assassination.'

They could hear an approaching

aircraft, but over the water where it would first appear, they could see nothing. The landing-lights did not reach quite that far.

The public address system directed the attention of all passengers to the departure, in fifteen minutes, of the airliner Buono had two reservations upon. It seemed that the imminent arrival of the City Attorney's aircraft was already past-tense. Germain wished this entire night were already past-tense as he straightened up and tried to fill out the lowering, bulky outline of an incoming airliner far out at the end of the landing area.

21

'The Place Is Secured'

The maintenance men went out and hovered, some near the fuel-lorry, some near a wheeled tractor with a low-bed luggage trailer attached to its tow-bar. Several men in coveralls with large rubber earphones clamped to their heads, were looking out where Germain finally detected the silvery shape. He turned as a large presence loomed behind him. It was Mallory looking bigger and more impassive than ever.

'We took the woman into custody,' he announced, without taking his eyes off the incoming airliner. 'No problems.'

Germain wondered. 'There'll be problems if he saw you do it.'

Mallory did not take his eyes off the aeroplane. 'He didn't. She went back to the rest-room. We nabbed her as she came out and took her next-door to an office.'

Mallory dropped his gaze to Germain. 'We're checking her out to tally the story, but my guess is that she's telling the truth. Buono picked her up in a bar, offered her three hundred dollars and a free flight up and back, to go with him.'

Germain was not surprised at all; sooner or later Buono would have jettisoned the flashy blonde. He might even have done it right there at the San Francisco airport, although it was more probable that he would have kept her with him until he was safely out of California.

The maintenance crew fired up its luggage-carrier and the fuel-lorry crept out to a yellow line and sat poised there. Men in the airline's distinct coveralls dropped cigarettes underfoot, and one of the men with earphones tested a pair of conical guidance-lights by flicking them on until the upper half glowed like torches, then he flicked them off again. He was the technician who signalled the pilot how close to taxi-in for the off loading of passengers and freight.

To Germain and the pair of detectives

standing with him, it was like watching a dress-rehearsal by actors who had been through it all hundreds of times before. It was also a little unreal; murder was imminent yet those men went about their work as though this was just another flight. Evidently the last one of the day for this particular crew, and their sole concern was in getting the airliner berthed, unloaded, and secured.

Germain asked Mallory if he shouldn't be upstairs with Sergeant Moore, and got a sardonic glance. 'He's setting things up.' Germain waited for an explanation but none came. The maintenance crew was moving into position out a hundred yards as the great airliner soughed in like a heavy wind, touched down with a screech that meant a hundred dollars worth of rubber had been burned off the tyres, and fled out of sight beyond the terminal building, where it would run out the momentum of landing, then turn and come lumbering back.

The public address system noted the approach of a flight from Omaha, giving the added information that this flight was twenty-four minutes late, and that passengers would disembark on the opposite side of the building.

Germain unbuttoned his jacket, not as any particular precaution but in order to give his hands something to do. A plain-clothes man approached Mallory and said, 'The crew will come off first.'

Mallory did not look either very enlightened or very pleased but he nodded, and the newcomer ran up the aerial of his hand-transceiver stepped out a few feet from the building and tested it. Germain was concentrating on the sound of the aircraft making its awkward sweep and turn as it left the flight-line and ponderously came towards the upper end of the terminal building. Madison popped chewing gum into his mouth and went to work on it while he also concentrated on the appearance of the jumbo-jet.

The man with those little orange cones lit them and moved farther out in order to see the aeroplane as soon as it appeared. He began signalling, first with one upraised torch, then with the other one, before Germain saw the aeroplane.

When the howling dropped a pitch and Hale Buchanan's aeroplane came round the building into Germain's sight, its ugly, round, blunt snout and thick, unlovely body made the building look out of proportion.

Up where the pilot and co-pilot sat behind their curved, tinted windscreen, there was light, but not enough to make out the men themselves. Farther back there was better light along both sides where portholes, like the breathing flukes of some prehistoric monster, quivered from vibration.

Germain spoke to Mallory without taking his eyes off the oncoming airliner. 'How good is Moore's net?'

Standing the same way, watching the aeroplane, Mallory said, 'Good enough, I suppose. It sure as hell *better* be good enough. No hacks will roll after this thing stops and the passengers get off, and no one will use an outside door in any part of the building.'

The detective with the transceiver suddenly raised the little instrument to the side of his head, listened a moment, then turned back where Germain and Mallory were standing.

'Sergeant Moore says the place is secured.'

Mallory gave the detective the same kind of sniffing look Germain felt like giving him.

'Secured for *what?*' asked Mallory, and the detective shrugged and went back out a short distance where his transceiver would function best.

The airliner had less than two hundred feet to go. Already, the men who operated the telescoping ramp that led from the aeroplane into the nearest lounge, were beginning to manually adjust their canopy. The ramp was like a hollow caterpillar; it was longer than the wing of the aeroplane in order to reach to the forward passenger-door; it was completely covered, and inside were spaced overhead lights. Disembarking people would scarcely realize they were off the aeroplane until, at the far end of the ramp, they were passed through two large glass doors into the lounge, except that the ramp tipped up just a little.

Moore would have men inside the covered ramp. In fact by now he would have men tightening their circle, sealing off the City Attorney's airliner from all outside interference as though it were landing a cargo of lepers.

Buono would have to make his attempt after the passenger-door was opened and before the ramp was secured to the passageway, or he would have to make his attempt upstairs in the lounge as the passengers stepped forth from the covered ramp.

Germain straightened up as the signalman with his little orange flares made a steady, forward motion, meaning that the aeroplane was on a direct coupling course with the ramp. He guessed that it might take the rampcrew two minutes to fix their caterpillar into place. During that time the door would be opened offering a good view of the aeroplane's interior, aft of the pilot's compartment.

When he was sure which way the aeroplane would turn in order to line up with the ramp, he left Mallory and the other detectives to stride briskly around to the far side of the aeroplane where the chalking-crew were standing ready to block the wheels.

Over there, on that side, a dozen or more maintenance men were busy. Germain studied each man between upward glances towards the imminent coupling. Each maintenance technician moved with the efficient assurance of a person who had done all this so many times before there was no need for hesitation.

Germain began to think Buono would make his attempt upstairs after all. Two men, one with earphones, one with a clipboard in his hand from which manifests fluttered in the chill air of midnight, were talking very earnestly. That was the only example of non-activity and it seemed entirely justified. Germain moved closer, got the luggage-trailer and tractor between himself and those two men, trying to get a better look at their faces while overhead a stewardess unbolted the bulk-head door and cracked it a little to look out, perhaps to help the ramp-men line up their folding caterpillar.

Germain put his right hand under his coat, turned and with his back to the doorway, looked for someone to step forth. It was now or never, from this angle. The man with the manifest-clipboard in his hands also turned to look back while his companion, the one with the earphones on his head, twisted slightly from the waist to keep an intent watch upon the ground-crew. No one was paying any attention to the aeroplane's upper structure from down below where the maintenance crew was working.

Very gradually, an agonizing inch at a time, the aeroplane minced ahead, in line with the off-loading ramp. The stewardess opened the door a bit wider and Germain saw the double chain snapped into place in front of her as she leaned to watch the ramp-men zero-in on the lighted opening. Behind her was someone wearing a jacket of autumn-tan. He was a fairly tall man with crinkly hair and a tanned face, beyond that Germain could make out nothing because a second man, equally tall but wearing blue, moved in, crowding the stewardess. Germain recognized this man the moment light touched his face: Berryman from the Intelligence Unit.

The aeroplane's intake began unwinding. A scuttling bright red wheel-tractor backed into place with a tow-bar jutting backwards. The driver was sitting twisted to watch the socket on the end of his drawbar line up with the ball of the forward leading gear. The red tractor would wheel the airliner the last few yards. For as long as all this was taking, the lighted interior of the aeroplane's cabin was clearly visible.

Germain ran a searching look among the ground-crewmen, none of whom showed any interest at all in the passengers above. He had now placed the man with the clipboard and his companion with the earphones. Despite their airline coveralls and their technical look, they were Moore's men.

Someone spoke above the unwinding sound of the jet engines and Germain swung. Jim Madison, the detective assigned to Germain, was coming over behind the luggage-trailer. At that moment the stewardess stepped away from the doorway and the man in the blue suit leaned out and downward. Germain verified that it was Berryman; he seemed to be making a close search of the area below the doorway, as though he expected someone to be down there. Germain could imagine who he was looking for. Madison started to speak, but Germain, watching the doorway again, saw Berryman flinch. At once the sound of a distant cork being popped from a champagne bottle brought Madison and Germain around towards the reinforced windows up along the high-rise of the airport building.

Germain yelled up for someone to close the bulkhead door. Berryman was already grappling with the parallel steel bar that served as the securing lock when the aeroplane was in flight. Behind him, the man in the autumn-tan jacket was standing up there as rigidly as a stone carving.

The unwinding jet engines were down to a hum by this time and the red tractor had made its hook-up. The driver eased ahead, his bug-like vehicle picking up slack and settling in the rear as it moved the giant aeroplane towards the ramp coupling.

Germain glimpsed the man with the earphones speaking swiftly into the tube that curved outwards and upwards in front of his chin. Nightmare-like, the attack was taking place in the midst of not less than thirty people who had no part in it, and who had no idea anything but just another routine bit of business was in progress.

Madison leaned and said, 'Where is it coming from?'

Germain did not know. 'In the building, up above,' was all he could say.

The inches-thick reinforced glass of the bulkhead doorway quivered in Germain's sight, then turned milky from impact. Berryman was fighting the heavy door while behind him the man in tan simply stood there. It would have been pointless for Germain to yell up for someone to help Berryman get the door closed. Even if they heard him, understood him, because not even the trim little steward-ess would have obeyed; she, like all the other people crowding up, had no idea someone was trying to kill the man in the autumn-tan jacket.

Madison yelled at someone and Germain turned; it was the detective with the transceiver, and Madison was telling him to tell the men upstairs that the assassin was in a room on the south side of the building overlooking the area where the airliner was being inched forward.

Berryman got the door halfway closed. Behind him, the man in tan half-turned towards the people pressing up from behind. When Germain swung to scan the rows of windows along the building, then back again, the man in tan was no longer in sight, but beyond the place where he had been standing, Germain clearly saw the postures of shock, of amazement, as those other passengers who had been crowding up, looked down towards the floor. Then Berryman slammed the bulkhead door and the little red tractor, completely unconcerned, rolled its loaded airliner up to where the ramp-men could make their connection.

It was all over.

Germain spun back towards the building and sprinted for the stairs. He did not know whether the other detectives were following him, and at the moment he did not care. Joe Buono had scored, Germain was sure of that. What remained now was to see whether Sergeant Moore's surround had really sealed off the entire second floor of the airport building, or not.

22

The Unlamented Passing

Sergeant Moore was in the lounge where the City Attorney was due to disembark. There were four men with him. A fifth man, new to Inspector Germain, was speaking with Moore when Germain hastened forward. The stranger turned and brushed past that young, swarthy airline official who was standing near the ramp's entrance, and disappeared down into the caterpillar-like covered ramp. Germain was lightly breathless from his rush to the upper floor, and also from the excitement. Mallory and the detective named Madison entered the lounge a moment or two behind him.

Three men, one with a transceiver, were with Sergeant Moore as Germain said, 'He's up here, Sergeant. He was firing from a south-side window somewhere.'

Moore nodded, unperturbed. 'I know.' He was about to say more when a brisk, younger man walked up, leaned and whispered to Moore, after which the sergeant looked around saw Mallory and Madison, and jerked his head. Without awaiting an explanation those two left the lounge with the brisk, younger man.

'He's cornered,' said Moore. 'And you were pretty close to being right, twice, Inspector. He tried the hit before anyone left the aircraft, and he is boxed-in down the corridor inside a rest-room.'

Germain, who had been equally interested in preventing murder, and in catching Buono, asked if Moore had contact with the aeroplane, and when Moore nodded, he then asked if Berryman had been hit, explaining that he had seen the man with Hale Buchanan wince.

Moore gave a dry reply. 'They both were. I was counting a little on the range being too great for a man using a revolver, and a silencer, but Buono is a damned good shot. Mr Buchanan wasn't hit directly though; the slug bounced off a metal strip above the door and angled downwards. It knocked him senseless when it ploughed alongside his head. I sent the doctor aboard just as you got up here.'

'Berryman?' asked Germain, and Moore permitted himself a thin, humourless smile.

'Caught two in the chest — on his flak-vest. He's all right. Shaken up but all right.' Moore gazed at the milling people who seemed to sense that something was badly wrong and were huddling the way bewildered people usually do. Moore jerked his head. 'Come on; Mr Buono is at bay and no one is very eager to rush into the rest-room and get him, including me.'

Germain walked out of the lounge into the wide corridor, which was actually an immense, long room that went down the back of the building behind all the separate lounges. There were uniforms in sight, finally, mostly blue S.F.P.D. uniforms, but also with a number of airport security guards in grey, placating people and answering questions; this sudden show of police force in the building was disrupting the usual ebb and flow of people; the curious ones crowded up to ask questions and the others gathered in little discreet clutches here and there, saying little and watching everything. It was the responsibility of the airport police to see that no bystanders interfered with the police, or were injured if there were serious trouble. They were equal to it, but right at the moment Germain was less aware of the people and the guards than he was of the professional city policemen and the plain-clothes men who were sealing off a closed metal door on the south side of the long wide corridor.

A greying man Germain had noticed before, mainly because he looked as old as Sergeant Moore, and as rugged, came over, nodded at Germain, and said, 'Nice situation, Sergeant.'

Moore accepted that assessment because it was in line with his own mood. 'Yeah.' As Moore stood gazing at the closed door the other man asked about the City Attorney and Berryman. Moore was laconic — and cynical. 'Berryman's all right. He was wearing his flak-vest. Buchanan's all right too, but he got a gouge alongside the head.' Moore and the other older man exchanged sardonic glances.

'Just what he needed,' said the other detective, 'to insure re-election. It'll be in the headlines tonight: Heroic City Attorney Survives Murderous Attack by Mafia Assassin.'

Germain would have smiled any other time at the total and unflappable cynicism of those two men, instead, he watched a plain-clothes man loading a gas-pistol with a small canister as the other officers stood by.

Moore also saw that, and looked at a man over beside the door. 'Have you told him to come out?' The man nodded. He was standing loosely but with one hand under his coat. Moore said, 'Try again,' and the detective turned slightly as he called out.

'Buono! You've got one last chance to come out, then we'll gas you out!'

The answer was prompt. 'Who's going to open the door to toss the gas can in?'

Moore, sounding tired, called to the cornered man. 'Come on, Buono, for God's sake; quit being an idiot. You're not going anywhere. We can stand out here for as long as it takes. Use your head.'

The answer was prompt again. 'Who are you?'

'I'm Sergeant Moore of Homicide. Now quit stalling and walk out of there.'

Buono said, 'No thanks. You come in and get me, Sergeant.'

Germain leaned. 'There's got to be an air-vent to that rest-room. Find out where it is, prise off the grille and drop the canister.'

Moore nodded and motioned Mallory over to give the instructions. As soon as Mallory walked away, taking the officer with the gas-pistol with him, Moore said, 'Buono? What's the point of all this? The best you can hope for is a Mexican stand-off for a few hours; you're through one way or the other.'

This time the answer was slower coming, and it occurred to Germain that the window from which Joe Buono had fired at the aeroplane was in the rear wall of the rest-room. Germain added something to what Moore had said.

'Joe? This is Inspector Germain of Chicago, where you iced that nut who planted the bomb on your flight to Denver. Listen, that damned window is two flights up from the tarmac. If you were lucky you'd get two broken legs. If you were unlucky, a broken neck or back, and the rest of your life in a wheelchair. Out front here is a little army of armed cops. Figure it out for yourself.'

Buono must already have figured it out because when he replied he didn't mention his chances. Instead, he said, 'Hey, Inspector; nice to talk to someone from Chicago. How'd you find out about the guy with the bomb?'

'We found him where you left him, in the parking area.'

'That doesn't mean I hit him, man.'

Germain agreed. 'It sure doesn't, but we ran you down — Mr Carlysle, Mr Bennington and Harrison. Listen to me, Joe: Scarpino put out a contract on you for not telling him you hit that nut in Chicago.'

'That's a lie,' spat Buono.

'It's the gospel truth,' called Sergeant Moore. 'He sent Mario Spina here to the airport to hit you. Mario hit a man who looked like you and we've got Mario. In case you want to think it over, Buono, here's something for you to mull over: Scarpino's powerful in the Council, as you know, and he won't let up just because we grabbed Mario. You're as good as dead right now, but if you walk out of there you'll get into maximum-security; that way we can keep you alive.'

Buono's answer dripped sarcasm. 'Beautiful. That's wonderful, Sergeant. Maximum-security until you've wrung me dry so you and that damned City Attorney I hit or his successor can make a case.'

Moore glanced at his watch, glanced down the room where Mallory and his companion had gone, and said, 'You didn't kill anyone; the City Attorney's nicked and the cop with him was wearing a flak-vest.'

Buono said, 'Flak-vest! Hey, Sergeant,

just how long have you guys been on to me?'

'Since you landed here, and flew north in that blue-and white helicopter,' said Moore, and turned a little irritably as a uniformed officer walked up and held out a folded slip of paper. Germain thought it was from Mallory, saying he was about to fill the rest-room with gas. He was never more wrong in his life, and he had a hint of that as he watched Sergeant Moore's face smooth out in surprise. Without a word Moore handed over the note, then called to Joe Buono again.

'Got a little news for you, Buono. Angelo Scarpino died an hour ago up there on his mountaintop.'

For a long, silent moment there was not a sound from beyond the rest-room door, then the cornered man said, 'What kind of a stupid trick is it, this time, Sergeant?'

'No trick,' called Germain, holding the note. 'Trying to eat everything in sight finally got to him, Joe. He had a heart attack up there. By the time Benny could get to that village near the highway to call for a doctor, he was dead. They're bringing him out now, in a helicopter.'

Joe Buono said no more, but Germain heard him cough, or sneeze, or make some kind of noise. Sergeant Moore glanced at his watch again, turned and gestured for everyone to get clear of the door. 'Maybe,' he told Germain, 'with nothing left, he'll come out shooting. Sometimes they react that way.'

The noise came again, identifiable as a cough. It was repeated several times, then they all heard Joe Buono begin to swear as he realized what was happening inside his glistening, tiled fortress.

He called Sergeant Moore a string of names, not a one of which Moore hadn't been called before since joining the police force. He included Allan Germain in the name-calling but it sounded as though his real animosity was against Moore.

A booming, guttural-sounding voice echoed from behind the rest-room door as Mallory, probably calling down through the air-vent, told Joe Buono to either walk out unarmed or more gas was coming.

The men outside, including Moore and Germain, scattered. Whatever Buono's intentions had been once, now, he only had one alternative to asphyxiation; surrender or death, but in either case he had to leave the rest-room.

The coughing became deeper and more pronounced. Germain finally lifted out his holstered sidearm, stood off to the far left of the door — because he thought Buono would be right-handed, and right-handed men usually looked right before they looked left — and waited.

That detective over against the wall beside the door pointed to a cloud-like vapour seeping from beneath the door and drew a handkerchief from his pocket to hold to his nose. It wasn't really a very effective kind of protection against gas, but the detective seemed determined not to leave his post. He also drew his revolver and held that loosely in his other hand.

Germain, watching this man as well as the door, saw the detective suddenly stiffen, whip his head around and lean as though listening. He called over.

'What did you hear?'

The detective glanced at Germain, then at his superior, Sergeant Moore. 'Sounded exactly like a silenced gunshot.'

Germain considered the implication a moment, then slowly put up his gun and moved forward. Moore called a warning, the other officers stood transfixed, watching in complete silence.

The gas was seeping steadily, at about ankle-height. It was heavier than air with a tendency to settle along the ground, or the lowest level. Germain picked up the first hint of its smell when he got over beside the door and gestured for the man standing there holding his handkerchief to his face to yield so that Germain could stand next to the door.

Germain did not call out. He reached carefully for the brass push-plate on the door, took a step closer in order to have more leverage, and very slowly and gingerly added more weight until the door began easing inward.

Mallory had not fired another canister or the room would have been like a cloud-bank. As it was, Moore had about three inches of opening to peer through where a milkiness like faint fog was everywhere. He got a fair smell that time because as the door opened the gas sought the opening.

He also saw what he had half-expected to see. Joe Buono lying crumpled, almost half-sitting, over against the glistening white-tiled far wall beyond a row of white washbasins, either dead or unconscious.

Germain let the door swing closed. Sergeant Moore was staring, waiting. So were all the other detectives and uniformed officers. 'His gun's lying in the middle of the room,' said Germain, 'and he's over against the north wall — down.'

Sergeant Moore strolled over. 'Dead?'

Germain did not know. 'There's blood, but that's all you can see. Anyone have a gas-mask? That's what it'll take to get him out of there.'

Moore, holding a handkerchief over his face, opened the door and looked in. For a full minute he stood looking before he let the door swing closed, and turned back to jerk his head towards the gas-filled room. 'Madison, go and tell Mallory it's over, not to waste another canister. Rob, call the meat wagon, he's dead.'

Germain was jolted but not surprised. Moore passed orders for the security of the building to be withdrawn. He took Germain with him back down where the passengers had finally disembarked from the airliner with Hale Buchanan on it, sat down and relaxed all over as he said, 'Well, in my book your Joe Buono was just another individual this world didn't need from the day he was born — but he kept the faith, didn't he? Buchanan and no one else will get from him what he knew about the Cosa Nostra. He kept his oath of secrecy. You know, Inspector, a man never has to admire his enemies, but the ones with guts, as you probably know from experience, sometimes earn your respect.'

Germain could agree, at least in part, with Moore's summary, but he felt that Buono might have surrendered if he had not been told that Angelo Scarpino had not only turned against him, but was also dead. Without Scarpino, even angry over what Buono had done, Joe Buono probably realized he did not have a chance of getting clear of the law this time.

Moore yawned. 'Well, what's next, Inspector?'

Germain had a ready answer. 'A shower, a big breakfast, then a long flight back to Chicago.'

Moore roused himself up out of the chair and thrust out a hand. He lent this gesture added sincerity by offering one of his smiles. 'Glad to have met you, Inspector, but do me a favour — don't come back to San Francisco until after I retire?'

They laughed together.

THE END

TURN DOWN AN EMPTY GLASS

Basil Copper

L.A. private detective Mike Faraday is plunged into a bizarre web of Haitian voodoo and murder when the beautiful singer Jenny Lundquist comes to him in fear for her life. Staked out at the lonely Obelisk Point, Mike sees the sinister Legba, the voodoo god of the cross-roads, with his cane and straw sack. But Mike discovers that beneath the superstition and an apparently motiveless series of appalling crimes is an ingenious plot — with a multi-million dollar prize.

DEATH IN RETREAT

George Douglas

On a day of retreat for clergy a
Overdale House, a resident guest,
Martin Pender, is foully murdered.
The primary task of the Regional
Homicide Squad is to track down the
bogus parson who joined the retreat.
Subsequent events show that serious
political motives lie behind the killing,
but the basic lead to it all is missing.
Then, three young tearaways corner
the killer in the woods, and a chess
problem, set out on a board, yields
vital evidence.

THE DEAD DON'T SCREAM

Leonard Gribble

Why had a woman screamed in Knightsbridge? Anthony Slade, the Yard's popular Commander of X2, sets out to investigate. Furthering the same end is Ken Surridge, a PR executive from a Northern consortium. Like Slade, Surridge wants to know why financier Shadwell Staines was shot and why a very scared girl appeared wearing a woollen housecoat. Before any facts can be discovered the girl takes off and Surridge gives chase, with Slade hot on his heels . . .